SOPHIE HARTLEY AND THE FACTS OF LIFE

Stephanie Greene

CLARION BOOKS
Houghton Mifflin Harcourt
Boston   New York

CLARION BOOKS

215 Park Avenue South
New York, New York 10003

Clarion Books is an imprint of Houghton Mifflin Harcourt Publishing Company.

www.hmhbooks.com

The text was set in New Baskerville.
Book design by Sharismar Rodriguez

Library of Congress Cataloging-in-Publication Data
Greene, Stephanie.
Sophie Hartley and the facts of life / by Stephanie Greene.
pages cm
Summary: "Sophie, 10, doesn't want to turn into a moody teenager like her
older brother and sister, and she certainly doesn't want to see the *movie*
(about gross adolescent body changes) at school. On the other hand, she doesn't
want to be considered immature by her classmates."—Provided by publisher.
ISBN 978-0-547-97652-5 (hardcover)
[1. Puberty—Fiction. 2. Maturation (Psychology)—Fiction.
3. Family life—Fiction.] I. Title.
PZ7.G8434So 2013
[Fic]—dc23   2012041489

Manufactured in the United States of America
DOC 10 9 8 7 6 5 4 3 2 1
4500439731

For Amy Radwan, who shrieked

ONE

"I hate my hair!"

Sophie took a pair of socks out of her top drawer and counted to herself silently. *One, one thousand . . . two, one thousand . . .*

"I HATE MY HAIR!" Her older sister, Nora, shouted it louder this time. Then she slammed the door of the bathroom cabinet before turning on the hair dryer full blast.

Even the hair dryer sounded furious.

Sophie sat on the end of her bed and reached for her sneakers. There once had been a time when the next thing to happen would have been Nora's storming into their room, hurling her hairbrush onto the dresser, and snarling, "Don't talk to me," before Sophie had even opened her mouth.

Then Sophie (the old Sophie) would have tried to cheer Nora up by saying something dumb like "I have curly hair, too, and I like it."

Sophie couldn't believe how much she'd matured in two short months.

Since Nora had moved up to the attic and Sophie had turned ten, Sophie had started seeing things in such a new light that she felt as if she could easily be eleven.

Or even twelve.

The thing was, Sophie wasn't in a rush to be eleven or twelve. It would bring her that much closer to being fourteen. After observing Nora for the past few months, Sophie had decided that fourteen was a very emotional age. She would have liked to keep a list of all the things that made Nora furious so she could start practicing not letting them bother her when *she* was fourteen. But ever since last year, when Sophie had discovered that everyone in the family had been reading her lists even though she'd kept them carefully hidden, she had given up lists.

One particular day last fall had made it final.

She and Nora were still sharing a room. Sophie was sitting at Nora's desk, intently reading something written in purple ink that she'd found in the desk drawer Nora had labeled KEEP OUT !, and didn't realize her sister had come in until Nora shrieked.

Then Sophie, who was so shocked by what she'd read that she completely forgot she'd taken the key to the drawer from its hiding place taped inside Nora's winter boot at the back of the closet, looked at her sister and said, "'Mr. and Mrs. Ian Bishop'? 'Mrs. Ian Bishop'? 'Nora Hartley Bishop'?

"Nora!" Sophie had cried. "You're *married?*"

Looking back, Sophie couldn't believe how young she'd been when she was nine. While Nora pounded on the door of the locked bathroom where Sophie had sought shelter, Sophie had sworn off lists for the rest of her life. Hers or anyone else's.

Lately, though, she wished she hadn't been so hasty. In order to remember everything, she had to walk around muttering, "Hair, boys, parties, nose, thunder thighs, Lisa Kellogg—hair, boys, parties, nose, thunder thighs, Lisa Kellogg," under her breath. Since the day Nora had overheard her and gotten mad about *that* because she said Sophie was making fun of her, Sophie had been forced to repeat that list in her head. Since her head was already crowded, it meant there was hardly any room left.

All she knew was that noses should be small, hair should be straight, and boys and parties were good unless they didn't like you or you didn't get invited to one. Then they were bad. She wasn't sure what Lisa Kellogg had done to make Nora hate her, or what thunder thighs were, but they were both definitely on the list. It was all very complicated.

What worried Sophie most of all, though, was something Nora had said a few weeks earlier. She and Mrs. Hartley had been arguing about a pair of expensive jeans that Nora said all the girls in middle school wore and Mrs. Hartley said they couldn't afford. Sophie was only trying to help when she said, "You should do what I do, Nora. Sew or glue things on your old jeans to make them look different."

"Butt out, Sophie," Nora said.

"Nora!" said Mrs. Hartley.

"It's none of her business."

"We're in the kitchen," Sophie said. "When you're having a conversation in the kitchen, anyone can join it."

"Oh, is that right?" Nora sneered at her in the way she'd perfected in middle school. "You think everything's so hunky-dory all the time. Just you wait, Little Miss Sunshine. *Your* time will come."

Nora had stormed up to her room before Sophie could ask exactly *when* Nora thought Sophie's time would come and what would happen to her when it did.

"She means you're going to become a teenager." Mrs. Hartley got up to put her mug into the dishwasher and muttered, "Heaven help us," under her breath.

"I heard that," said Sophie. "It doesn't help, on top of Nora."

"Sorry." Her mother flashed a fake smile. "Who knows, Sophie? Maybe you'll be the first adolescent in history to become a teenager who doesn't have temper tantrums or grow a mustache!"

"You know I won't," Sophie said gloomily. "Even Thad changed. Remember how he suddenly grew hair all over his arms and legs and went around giving us beard burns and flapping his arms to show off his hairy underarms?"

"Please." Her mother picked up her briefcase and started for the hall. "Three teenagers in one house," she said. "What were we thinking?"

It wasn't very comforting.

What if Nora was right and Sophie had no other choice than to become a teenager who burst into tears one minute and was hysterical with happiness the next? And who argued with almost everyone in her family?

Sophie didn't want to become that kind of person. For one thing, she didn't like to argue. For another, she liked the people in her family. Now that she was fourteen, Nora seemed to hate most of them. She ignored Sophie whenever she could and argued with everyone else, almost every day.

Mr. Hartley was safe because he was on the road so much of the time, and Maura still talked in one- or two-word sentences. Even Nora couldn't argue with a toddler who said only "Wow!" and "Okay!" As for John, he had a way of ignoring everything that went on above his head. Since he was seven and short, he managed to avoid most family arguments.

Nora argued constantly with Thad and their

mother. Her temper had started to affect everyone in the family. Mrs. Hartley had been much grouchier than usual lately. After she and Nora had had a particularly heated argument one afternoon, Sophie found her mother in the family room, pacing back and forth and muttering, "Be the rock . . . Be the rock . . ."

"What rock?" Sophie asked.

"Mothers are meant to be the rock their children build their lives on," Mrs. Hartley said grimly. "On days like this, I feel more like sand."

Now, as if on cue, Sophie heard the bathroom door open and Nora shout, "Thad, if you use my deodorant one more time, I'm going to kill you!" as she stomped past Sophie's door on her way back up to the attic. Sophie finished tying her shoes and stood up. If she couldn't avoid fourteen entirely (and the only way to do it that she'd come up with was both painful and permanent), she needed to start practicing what not to get annoyed about, right away.

She went over to her art table to take a last-minute look at the collage she was making. Her class had learned how to make collages. Sophie loved cutting pictures out of magazines and words out of newspapers, and collecting anything that grabbed her attention when she was outside, to put on them. Some kids laughed at how Sophie's collages had things sticking out, but she liked them that way.

They were interesting.

She was working on a collage for Alice now. Alice had fallen in love with tie-dyeing a few months earlier, after her mother had bought her a kit. She had tie-dyed T-shirts and belts and hats with different-colored swirls and stripes. She had made an artist apron for Sophie and tie-dyed swirls in different colors all over it. Sophie had based her collage for Alice on tie-dyeing and pasted on color swatches and photographs and all kinds of other things. She had found a small spring, painted it blue, and pasted that on to represent a swirl.

All she needed now was a photograph of Alice to put in the middle. Or maybe a picture of Alice with her and Jenna.

When Sophie heard Thad go downstairs, she realized she was late and quickly checked herself in the mirror on her closet door. Her hair looked ratty in the back, even for her. She'd neglected to take out her ponytail before she went to bed last night. Now a piece of the yellow yarn she'd used in her collage was tangled up in it.

Sophie picked up her hairbrush and then stopped.

Nope, she thought firmly, putting it back down. Not worrying about hair was number one on her list. There had to be a positive way of looking at the snarled mess on the back of her head.

She studied it critically from several angles.

If she used her imagination, the mess looked a bit like the bird's nest John had found last summer and kept on his bookshelf. *Cool.* If she could find a real feather on the way to school, her hair would look exactly like a nest. And since hers didn't have a crushed egg in it, she didn't have to worry it was going to smell bad, either.

Sophie picked up her kitten, Patsy, from where she was sleeping on the bed, and went down to breakfast.

TWO

"Red alert," Sophie said as she walked into the kitchen. "Nora's having a bad hair day."

"So what else is new?" said Thad. He tore off a piece of his untoasted bagel with his teeth, quickly checked to make sure his mother's back was turned, and took a slug of milk from the container before putting it back in the refrigerator. "When's the last time she had a *good* hair day?"

"Not one word about it when Nora comes down, please," Mrs. Hartley told him. "I'd like to get this day off to a peaceful start."

"Not even an *a*?" John was carefully arranging slices of banana on a piece of bread smeared with peanut butter and didn't look up. "*A*'s a word."

The Hartley children had been responsible for making their own breakfasts since January, when Mrs. Hartley had switched from part-time to full-time as a home health care nurse. She'd said she was tired of the way they complained about what she made for them anyway, so except for Maura, "you can all take care of yourselves from now on." The only rules were that they had to fix something nutritious and eat at the table.

Breakfast had become much more peaceful. They all ate the same things every day.

Peanut butter and banana sandwich for John.

Cheese and untoasted bagel for Thad ("Why heat it up when it's only going to cool down in my stomach?"). Sophie opted for cold cereal, and Nora ate yogurt.

Maura was easy. She ate anything that was put in front of her.

Or left on the floor.

Last week, Sophie had discovered Maura on her hands and knees in the mudroom, eating the food in Patsy's bowl. Sophie had always wondered what cat food tasted like but had never had the nerve to try it herself. She wished Maura could really talk so she could describe it.

It had to taste better than the oatmeal their

mother had cooked for Maura this morning. Sophie felt her mouth puckering up when her mother said, "Yum, yum!" and put a bowl of it in front of Maura.

"Mom, you're brainwashing her!" Sophie said.

Maura said only, "Okay!" and dug in with her spoon.

"I hope the cat food killed her taste buds," said John.

"Yeah, Mom, really," Thad said. "Forcing that stuff on a defenseless child."

Sophie reached into the box of cereal she'd grabbed and took a handful. "Sophie, sit at the table, please, and use a bowl. You know better." Their mother was now cutting up an apple for Maura and didn't turn around. "And Thad . . . get a glass."

"I'm done." Thad popped the last piece of bagel into his mouth and brushed the crumbs off his hands over the sink. "No mess, no fuss. You don't even have to clean up after me."

"How considerate of you," said Mrs. Hartley.

"I don't know why you're so formal," Thad said, lifting his letter jacket off the back of a chair. "Everyone I know eats on the bus or when they get to class."

"I know. And does homework on the bus and puts on makeup," their mother said. "I guess we're a proper, old-fashioned family. You're lucky I don't make you wear a tie to breakfast."

Sophie put the cereal box and a bowl on the table and sat down.

"What's with girls and their hair, anyway?" Thad asked.

"'Girls'?" Nora echoed, coming into the room. She put her stack of books on the counter before she headed for the refrigerator. "*Who* had the fit last week because John used up his foam mousse?"

"Give me a break," said Thad. "He used it as snow around his Lego fort. Emily paid twelve bucks for that can."

Emily was Thad's new girlfriend. His "girlfriend of the month," as Nora called her. Nora said Emily was the kind of girl whose parents bought her a new SUV after she rolled the first one and who got a manicure every two weeks. Since Nora complained about the Hartleys' used car all the time and spent most of her babysitting money on manicures, Sophie would have thought Nora would admire Emily.

All Sophie knew was that since Thad had started going out with Emily, he'd been paying a lot more attention to his clothes and hair. Luckily, he didn't cry about them.

"Emily got cheated," John said. "It only lasted a few minutes."

"Nice hair, Nora," said Thad.

Nora gave her head a self-conscious shake.

"Too bad it's starting to rain."

Nora checked the window over the sink, shrieked, and ran back upstairs.

"Thad, really!" Mrs. Hartley snapped. "You're sixteen years old! When are you going to be mature enough not to say every single inflammatory thing that comes into your head!"

"What?" Thad protested. "It *is* starting to rain." A horn honked in the driveway. Thad picked up his gym bag, said, "Emily's here—got to go," and bolted. The mudroom door slammed behind him.

In the silence that followed, Mrs. Hartley looked up at the ceiling and sighed. "Is it asking too much for *one* of my children to exhibit a bit of self-control?" she said. "I don't expect it all the time, but every once in a while?"

Sophie didn't say anything. When she was little, she'd thought her mother was addressing God when she talked to the ceiling. Now she knew Mrs. Hartley was talking to herself. Sophie had learned (the hard way) that the safest policy was to stay quiet and let the moment pass.

Besides, even if she *could* think of a time when she'd exhibited self-control lately and told her mother about it, Nora would probably overhear her and call her "Little Miss Sunshine." She called Sophie that so often that she'd shortened it to "LMS."

Sophie had to work hard not to show how annoying it was.

"One time, even?" Mrs. Hartley pleaded.

"Okay!" said Maura.

Mrs. Hartley laughed. "Thank you, Maura. It's nice to know one of my children listens to me. You don't talk back, either." Mrs. Hartley gave Maura a loud kiss and unsnapped her bib. "Sophie, if you're finished, would you go and see if your father wants anything before I leave?"

Sophie put her bowl into the dishwasher and headed for the stairs.

"And tell him that one tiny broken bone doesn't mean he can't get up and dressed!" her mother called.

Sophie went up the stairs and down the hall to her parents' bedroom.

Mr. Hartley had arrived home unexpectedly three days before. He was supposed to be moving a family to Florida, but one of the men who worked for him had dropped a couch on Mr. Hartley's foot. It had broken a small bone. Now Mr. Hartley had to wear a plastic boot for ten days and couldn't drive or lift heavy things.

At first, everyone in the family had been happy to see him. They weren't used to having him around for ten whole days. Except for a week during the summer and at Christmas, Mr. Hartley spent only two or three days at home between jobs.

It wasn't long, however, before the fact that all he did was lie on the couch in his sweatpants, reading or watching TV and calling for people to bring him things, had gotten on Mrs. Hartley's nerves.

Last night after dinner, when they'd been watching one of their favorite programs in the family room, Mr. Hartley had asked if someone would make him a sandwich. Sophie started to get up, but her mother held out her hand. "Stay," she ordered. "Your father isn't so wounded that he can't fix his own snack."

"I don't mind," Sophie said.

"Sit."

Sophie sat. "I don't see why you hate the idea of having a dog so much," she grumbled. "It would be well behaved with *you* around."

"Thank you, Sophie, but your mother's right," her dad said. "I can make it myself."

Nora snorted when Mr. Hartley made a brave show of struggling to his feet and limping into the kitchen.

"Where do you keep your bread?" he called after a few minutes.

"*My* bread?"

Sophie and Nora exchanged glances.

"Why is it *my* bread?" Mrs. Hartley shouted. "Perhaps if you made your own sandwiches more often, you'd know where we keep *the* bread!"

There was silence in the family room except for the sound of the TV until Mr. Hartley reappeared in the doorway. "And where, pray tell," he asked in an innocent voice, "do you keep your mayonnaise?"

Sophie saw the mayonnaise jar tucked inside his shirt and had to cover her mouth so she wouldn't laugh. When they were little and lost something like a sock or a shoe or a mitten, their dad would show up with the item hanging from an ear or perched on top of his head and say, "I wonder where it can be." It always made them laugh.

Last night, Mrs. Hartley hadn't cracked a smile.

"Dad?" Sophie called now as she got near her parents' bedroom door.

"Come in!"

Her father was dressed and sitting on their bed. Sophie sat down beside him.

"Was that Nora I heard running back up to her room?" he asked.

"It's raining," Sophie said. "She blew dry her hair straight."

Her dad looked at her.

"Nora hates her curly hair."

"I'm afraid she got that hair from my mother," he said.

Mr. Hartley's mother had died before Sophie

was born. Her dad kept a wedding picture of his mother and father on his dresser. Sophie and Nora used to prop it up when they played with their dollhouse and pretend their grandparents were the dolls' parents. Nora had named them Mr. and Mrs. Witherspoon because she thought it sounded fancy.

Sophie glanced at the framed photo now. It could have been Nora in the picture.

"Nora likes to blame it on Mom," Sophie said. "She wants to get her hair straightened, but Mom says it's too expensive."

"Let me guess," Mr. Hartley said. "Thad was the one who pointed out it was raining."

"Right."

"I'm catching on."

"You are," said Sophie. "Nora argues with everyone these days."

"I'm afraid our Nora's going through a prickly patch," her dad said. "It's her age."

"Does everyone fight when they're teenagers?"

"Not necessarily. I didn't. But I only had one brother, your uncle Pete. He was a lot older, so I looked up to him."

"Like John and Thad."

"Exactly." Her dad patted her knee. "Don't worry. I don't think you'll be a fighter, Sophie. You're a glass-half-full kind of person."

"Don't say that around Nora. It'll make her mad." Sophie stood up. "Need me to tell you where Mom keeps her coffee?"

Her dad laughed and reached out to tousle her hair, but Sophie ducked. "Don't touch it," she said. "I want it the way it is."

"It looks as if you have a family of mice in there."

"Close."

"I'm afraid yours is going to curl, too, if it's raining," her dad said.

"The curlier the better," Sophie said firmly.

THREE

Jenna and Alice were waiting for Sophie in front of the school. The three of them had been walking into the building together since they'd become best friends at the beginning of second grade.

Jenna was holding her iridescent orange yo-yo. It was her newest hobby. She carried it everywhere.

"Watch this," she said as Sophie came up to them. Jenna jerked her hand back and sent the yo-yo down the string. It hovered above the pavement, spinning, until she jerked her hand again. The yo-yo sped back up the string and settled neatly into her palm.

The girls started into the building.

"Isn't that cool?" Jenna said. "It's called 'sleeping the yo-yo.'"

"I tried the yo-yo when Thad had one, but I stunk," said Sophie.

"The trick I'm learning now is even better," Jenna said. "It's called 'walk the dog.' Wait till you see it."

"You've got something in your hair, Sophie," Alice said, reaching out.

"Don't touch it!" said Sophie. She covered the delicate gray feather she'd found on the sidewalk with her hand. "I want it there. It's supposed to look like a bird's nest."

"On purpose?" said Alice. "What'd your mom say?"

"My mom's bored with hair," Sophie said as they went into the school. "Nora cries all the time about hers being curly, and Maura screams whenever Mom tries to comb hers. Mom probably wishes we were all bald."

"My mom says we're at the age when we need to start thinking about hygiene," said Alice. "If I wore a feather in my hair, she'd have a fit."

"What's hygiene?" said Jenna.

"You know, wearing deodorant and things like that," Alice said. She blushed. "She bought me a deodorant called Summer Breeze. It smells pretty."

"I wish your mom would talk to some of the boys in our class," said Jenna. "Especially after recess."

"You're wearing deodorant?" Sophie said. "Let me smell." She leaned forward, sniffing Alice like a dog. "Summer Breeze . . . I smell barbecued hot dogs."

"Sophie! You're embarrassing me," Alice said, pushing her away.

"You get embarrassed about everything," said Jenna. She was making the yo-yo travel up and down the string while they walked. "Next Halloween, you could wear brown and go trick-or-treating as a tree, Sophie," she said. "And if you found a whole bird's egg, you could put that in your nest. Or maybe a hard-boiled egg, so it wouldn't break."

"Good idea," said Sophie. "I could wear green gloves for leaves."

"I might go as an Olympic yo-yo champion," Jenna said.

"I don't think they have yo-yos in the Olympics."

"They should," Jenna said. "They have Ping-Pong."

"Next year, we get to go to the fifth-grade Halloween dance," said Alice.

Sophie and Jenna looked at her.

"What? It's supposed to be a lot of fun," Alice protested.

"More fun than getting free candy?" said Sophie.

"Nothing's more fun than getting free candy," said Jenna.

Sophie had a flashback to the night the week before when Nora had found out that a girl she knew was having a party and she, Nora, hadn't been invited. "Take it from me. All dances and parties do is make girls cry," she said. "Boys make them cry, too."

"Boys don't cry, but girls and parties sure make them act weird," said Jenna, who had three older brothers.

They turned in to the hallway to Mrs. Stearns's room. A group of girls was clustered outside one of the fifth-grade classrooms. One of them whispered something that made the rest of them shriek. Destiny, another fourth grader, broke away from the group when she spotted Sophie, Jenna, and Alice and hurried toward them.

"Uh-oh, bad news," Sophie said. "Either that or something mean."

Last year, the three of them had decided Destiny was a snob. At the beginning of fourth grade, she was nice to Jenna because they were on the same lacrosse team. But when Destiny wanted everyone on the team to wear a ponytail and Jenna refused, Destiny had unfriended her.

The three of them had gone back to thinking she was a snob.

"Darn!" Jenna said now. Her yo-yo dangled lifelessly near the floor. She stopped to wind it back up.

"Guess what?" Destiny said breathlessly, rushing up to Sophie and Alice.

"What?"

Destiny looked around to make sure no one was listening. "The fifth-grade girls are going to see *the movie* next week," she whispered. She stood back and slapped her hands over her mouth as if to suppress a shriek. Her eyes were huge.

"What movie?" said Sophie.

"You're kidding! You don't know about *the movie?*" Destiny's hands dangled at her sides and her mouth dropped open as if Sophie had just said the most ridiculous thing she'd ever heard. Sophie was glad she had so much practice in not showing when she was annoyed.

"Sophie . . ." Alice said.

"I know about a lot of movies," Sophie told Destiny. "Which one are they seeing?"

"Sophie . . ." Alice tugged at Sophie's sleeve.

"What?!"

Alice looked as if she were ready to die of embarrassment. Her face and neck were bright red. "It's not that kind," she whispered.

"See?" Destiny said with a flick of her hair. "Even *Alice* knows."

It took all of Sophie's self-control to pretend she hadn't noticed that Destiny was insulting both her and Alice and to say calmly, "So, what kind is it?"

"It's about . . . you know . . ." Alice fluttered her hands nervously up and down in front of her chest and stomach. "Your *body*."

"What about it?"

"You know . . . how it changes and everything."

"Oh." Sophie suddenly thought about the book

Mrs. Hartley had bought for Nora a few years ago. As soon as she'd gotten it, Nora had started acting secretive and private, even undressing in the bathroom when she'd always changed in front of Sophie before. Nora had told Sophie the book was about "your *body*," in the same kind of voice Alice had just used, and said that Sophie was too young to look at it. Whenever her friends came for a sleepover, Nora said they had "girl business" to discuss and locked Sophie out of their room. Sophie had pressed her ear to the keyhole many times, but all she'd ever heard was whispering and giggling.

The way Alice was blushing and squirming now, giggling wasn't far behind.

"We don't care about that stuff," Sophie told Destiny.

"Alice does." Destiny looked pointedly at Alice and said, "Hailey's older sister saw the movie last year and said it was *disgusting*."

"If it's a disgusting movie, my brothers have probably seen it." Jenna slipped the yo-yo into her pocket as she joined them. "That's the only kind of movie they like to watch."

"Your *brothers* saw the movie?" Destiny clapped

her hands over her mouth again and then shrieked, "That is *so* embarrassing! Wait till I tell Hailey!"

She rushed over to a dark-haired girl who was wearing the same exact headband Destiny wore and grabbed her hands.

"Why is that so embarrassing?" Jenna said as they continued down the hall.

"Destiny was talking about the movie the fifth-grade girls are watching next week," Sophie said. "Boys don't watch it."

"It's about *poo-berty*," Alice whispered excitedly.

"My brothers joke about that all the time, except they say *pew-berty*," said Jenna.

"I hate that word," said Sophie.

"It's too embarrassing to say out loud," said Alice.

"If you ask me, it should be *P-U-berty*." Sophie pinched her nose shut. "I'm sick of the whole thing."

"You sound so funny." Alice giggled. She pinched her nose, too, and said, "P-U-berty."

"You can say that again," Jenna said. "P-*U*-berty."

They burst out laughing. It was a relief, saying

it that way. It made the idea feel funny instead of embarrassing.

"I have an idea." Sophie halted when they got near their classroom. "Only the three of us will say it like that. Every time anyone else says it the other way, or even talks about it, we'll look at one another and remember it."

"Right. And raise our eyebrows the way Mrs. Stearns does, but we won't say a word," Jenna added. "It'll be our secret signal."

She raised her eyebrows until they almost disappeared under her bangs. Sophie raised hers, too. Alice tried, but all that happened was that her eyes opened wide while her eyebrows moved so close together, they were almost touching. Sophie and Jenna laughed harder.

"Sounds like an interesting conversation," Mrs. Stearns said as she swept past them on her way into their classroom. "Time to come in, ladies."

The girls trooped in, giggling, behind their teacher. Sophie covered her mouth with her hands and wiggled excitedly. "'Your brothers saw the *mooooo-vie?*'" she mimicked. "Destiny's so ridiculous. She acts like she's so much older than us."

"She *is* older than us," Jenna said. "When we played lacrosse, Destiny thought she should be the captain because she's supposed to be in the fifth grade. She said it wasn't fair her parents kept her back in kindergarten."

"Not fair to us, you mean," said Sophie.

"Boys and girls," called Mrs. Stearns. "Before we go to lunch, I have an announcement."

Several of the boys slammed their books shut and stood up, ready to bolt at the sound of their teacher's voice. Mrs. Stearns shook her head at them and said, "Stay seated for a minute, please."

There was a lot of grumbling as they settled back down.

"Starting next week," Mrs. Stearns said when the room was quiet, "the fourth grade is going to be given an alternative to your usual gym class."

"Video games?" Matt Majercik said hopefully.

"Nice try, Matt." Mrs. Stearns looked around the room. "As part of a special program, Ms. Bell, the guidance counselor, is going to teach you yoga twice a week for a month. She teaches a children's course on the weekends."

"Yoga's for girls," David O'Neill said disgustedly.

"No, yoga is for everyone," said Mrs. Stearns. "Football players do yoga. It can greatly improve your balance, your coordination, and your flexibility."

"What's that?" the girl behind Sophie asked.

"Touching your toes," said Sophie.

"I can touch my toes—easy." Across the aisle, Caleb lifted up his foot and touched the end of his sneaker. "See?"

"Sophie and Caleb." Mrs. Stearns waited for a moment before she went on. "People, it's important to keep an open mind about this. According to Mr. Duncan, yoga is a lot of fun and not hard to do."

Another class groan.

Mr. Duncan was the gym teacher. Every year at the beginning of the national physical fitness month, he told them that climbing to the ceiling while holding on to a rope in each hand was fun too.

"Yoga helps create a feeling of inner peace and harmony," Mrs. Stearns went on, "and can help people develop *self-control.*"

Sophie could have sworn Mrs. Stearns fixed her

with a beady eye when she said that part, but maybe not. Sophie knew she wasn't the only one in her class who had a problem with self-control. Almost everyone in the fourth grade could have done with a lesson.

"I'm going to leave this sign-up sheet on the corner of my desk," Mrs. Stearns said, waving a piece of paper in the air. "If you want to try yoga, sign it. If you don't, you'll play volleyball for the next four weeks."

"I'm doing volleyball," Jenna said when everyone stood up to get in line. "My brothers are the ones who should take yoga if it's good for self-control."

"I don't like all the jumping up and down you have to do in volleyball," said Alice. "It feels like my brain's rattling around inside my head."

Sophie didn't like volleyball, either. Ever since the time she'd gotten bonked on the head in third grade, she couldn't help but duck when the ball came anywhere near her. It made the kids on her team mad. And since her mother had wished for one of her children to show self-control only this morning, yoga couldn't start a minute too soon.

Sophie was the first one to sign up.

FOUR

Sophie offered to read to Maura before dinner that night. She liked reading to Maura. She got to revisit picture books she'd loved when she was little without Nora saying, "Aren't you a little old for that?"

Sophie was convinced she could teach Maura to talk in full sentences if she read to her enough, too. Her mother didn't seem at all worried that Maura barely talked. She said Maura would do it in her own time. But Alyssa, a girl in Sophie's class, had a two-year-old sister, and Alyssa said she talked nonstop.

Right now, Sophie was reading Maura her favorite book for the third time. It was about a mouse that was afraid of the wind during a storm because it thought the wind was the voice of an invisible monster.

When Sophie got to the end, Maura took her

thumb out of her mouth long enough to say, "Again."

Sophie started again. She nearly had the words memorized. "'"Please be quiet," the tiny mouse squeaked,'" she read in a high-pitched mouse voice. Then, in a deep voice, "'But the wind wouldn't be quiet. It moaned and groaned. It rattled and roared.'

"'"YOU GREAT BIG BULLY!" the tiny mouse squeaked,'" Sophie read. "'"WHY DON'T YOU PICK ON SOMEONE YOUR OWN SIZE!"'"

Sophie always shouted this line. Maura got excited every time. She bounced up and down now in Sophie's lap and clapped her hands.

"Come on, Maura," Sophie said encouragingly. "You say it with me this time. '"You great big bully!"'"

Maura only laughed.

Before Sophie had to read the book all the way through for the fourth time, Mrs. Hartley called them to dinner. Sophie and Maura arrived in the kitchen with Thad and John hard on their heels. Mr. Hartley was standing at the counter, opening the lids of two boxes containing large pizzas.

"I'd hardly call that 'preparing dinner,'" Mrs.

Hartley was saying as she took plates out of the cabinet and put them on the counter.

"He had it delivered, too," Nora said.

"Whose side are you on?" said Mr. Hartley.

"Don't knock it, Nora." Thad helped himself to two slices. "It beats his world-famous chicken chow mein."

In the past, whenever Mrs. Hartley had gone away for a night and left their father in charge, Mr. Hartley had immediately bought the largest can of chicken chow mein he could find, heated it up, and poured it over dry Chinese noodles.

Luckily, she left them for only one night at a time.

"That stuff looks like spiders in slime," said John.

Sophie thought that was a perfect description, but she felt sorry for her dad. She thought it was nice that he'd offered to fix dinner. Nothing he did these days seemed to make their mother happy.

"Chow mein's not so bad," she said loyally.

"'Chow mein's not so bad,'" Nora mimicked. Then, under her breath, "LMS."

"What's 'LMS'?" said John.

"Nora's swearing at me," Sophie told him.

"Nora said a swear, Nora said a swear," John sang.

"Nora," Mrs. Hartley said tiredly.

Nora rolled her eyes and carried her plate to the table.

"'That stuff' is bean sprouts, John, and they're good for you." Mr. Hartley sat down at one end of the table. "You children are getting to be an ungrateful bunch."

"What have I been trying to tell you?" said Mrs. Hartley. She put a bowl of salad on the table and sat down at the other end.

Sophie looked from her mother to her father. They sounded as if they were agreeing and arguing at the same time.

"Guess what I signed up for today in school?" Sophie said. "Yoga. It's supposed to be good for self-control." She looked hopefully at her mother, but Mrs. Hartley was busy putting salad onto John's plate.

"You, taking yoga? That's a joke," Nora said. "It involves exercise. You realize that?"

"I know it does," Sophie said.

"You stink at exercise," Nora said.

"Yoga's different."

"Tae kwon do's better," said John.

John had started taking lessons at the White Tiger Tae Kwon Do Center near his school. He practically lived in his white uniform. The top had a drawing of a snarling tiger on the back.

John was up to his yellow belt and proud of it. He'd even started referring to himself as "White Tiger." Whenever anyone in the family got mad, John would place the palms of his hands together, bow slightly, and say, "White Tiger says, 'Do not use angry words.' White Tiger says, 'Use hands and feet.'"

They'd all quickly learned that even though he was skinny, John's bony feet could hurt when strategically directed at their shinbones.

"I'm learning how to break a board in half," John announced.

"Why would anyone want to break a board?" said Nora. She was methodically cutting her pizza into neat squares. "You're a nut basket, John."

"Yeah, and like he's the only one in the family," said Thad.

"Don't be so hard on yourself, Thad," Nora said.

"Please." Mr. Hartley held up his hand. "Could we get through one dinner without any bickering? I've had four nights of it in a row. I find I have a low tolerance for it."

"And I don't?" The arctic winds in their mother's voice wafted over the table. Judging from the look on her face, that wasn't a good thing for Mr. Hartley to have said. "Do you think I like it, having to listen to this all the time," Mrs. Hartley said to him, "while you're blissfully alone on the road somewhere?"

"Blissfully alone"? Wasn't that insulting to the children?

"Alone in the cab of my truck or in a motel with paper-thin walls, you mean?" said Mr. Hartley. "I'd hardly call that 'blissful.'"

"At least you're alone."

That was *definitely* insulting to the children. Sophie looked at Nora and Thad for confirmation, but they kept their heads down.

"It wasn't so bad when they were younger," Mrs.

Hartley went on, as if "they" weren't sitting there listening. "I could send them up to their rooms. Now look at them."

Her parents actually turned and looked at them. Sophie was shocked. They didn't look at John and Maura, only at Sophie and Nora and Thad. One at a time, too. Long, pointed looks that were decidedly unfriendly.

It was Mr. Hartley who finally broke the silence. "I guess we have to keep them," he said.

"I suppose so," Mrs. Hartley said with a sigh. "Who else would take them?"

"Mom!" Sophie said. "That's not very nice!"

"Is this what they refer to as a 'warm family moment'?" said Nora.

"I think we should *all* take yoga," Sophie said indignantly. "Then maybe *no one* would say every flammatory thing that came into their head."

"That's *in*flammatory, Soph," said Thad.

"I'm not being inflammatory," said Mrs. Hartley. "I'm making an observation."

"Yeah, a mean one," said Sophie.

The phone rang as they were clearing the table.

Nora raced to get it. "Sophie!" she yelled. "It's for you!"

Sophie picked up the phone in the family room and said, "Hello?"

"Destiny called me," Alice said breathlessly.

"She did?" said Sophie. "What did she want?"

There was a short silence. Then Alice said, "She said she really, really liked the tie-dyed belt I wore last week."

"'Really, *really*'?" Sophie repeated. "So, why's Destiny being so nice all of a sudden?"

"I don't know. She also said . . . well . . . don't get mad, Sophie, but she said she was scared about the movie but she was excited, too," Alice said. "She wanted to know if I wanted to come to her meeting."

"Destiny's holding a meeting?" Sophie said. "What for?"

"One of her friends is going to tell her what's in the movie and Destiny's going to tell us." Alice sounded miserable.

"That's ridiculous. You know what she's trying to do, don't you?"

Nora came into the room and frowned when

she saw Sophie was still on the phone. "Sophie . . ." she hissed furiously. "Get off! I'm expecting a call."

For once, Sophie was glad to do what Nora told her.

"I've got to go," she said to Alice. "I'll talk to you tomorrow."

The nerve of Destiny, Sophie fumed as she went up to her room. Holding a meeting about the movie. What an idiot. Sophie wished they'd never heard about the movie and that there was no such thing as P-U-berty.

"Patsy, get off!" she said grouchily to her kitten. She lifted Patsy off the pile of clean clothes her mother had left at the foot of Sophie's bed and dropped her onto the rug. Then Sophie immediately felt remorseful and picked her up again.

"I don't know why I'm blaming you." Sophie squeezed Patsy to her chest until Patsy let out a tiny mew. "Sorry," said Sophie, and put her gently back onto the pile. "Just be glad you're not a person."

She took her homework papers out of her backpack and dropped the pack onto the floor. That

Destiny! She was obviously trying to steal Alice, and Alice was too nice to suspect anything.

Sometimes it was so frustrating, the way Alice insisted everyone was good. Why, if Sophie had her way—

Sophie stopped herself.

Oh, no. It was happening.

She was acting about Destiny the way Nora acted about Lisa Kellogg. Lisa had annoyed Nora since they were in the fifth grade. For three whole years, Nora had been letting Lisa upset her. It was ridiculous! Sophie was *not* going to let Destiny bug her the same way.

"Did Alice tell you Destiny called her last night?" Sophie asked Jenna when she joined her and Alice in front of the school the next morning. Alice immediately looked guilty.

"What for?" said Jenna.

She and Sophie both looked at Alice.

"She just wanted to talk about the movie," Alice said meekly.

"Tell her the rest, Alice," Sophie said. To Jenna:

"She invited Alice to a meeting she's going to have to tell everyone about the movie."

"That's dumb. She doesn't even like you, Alice," Jenna said. "You aren't going, are you?"

"Of course not," Alice said unhappily. "Not if you and Sophie aren't invited."

When it was time for yoga that morning, the girls who had brought sweatpants from home were allowed to change in the girls' room. Ms. Bell was talking to Mr. Duncan when they got to the gym. She was dressed in black pants and a T-shirt. "Everyone grab a mat and sit down," she called as they filed in. "Space out your mats. Give yourselves plenty of room."

Sophie grabbed one of the blue mats from a pile at the front and put it on the floor near the bleachers. The mat was thick and spongy. It was fun to have her own space. Kids from each of the three fourth-grade classes were putting down their mats all around the gym floor. Destiny and Hailey put theirs in the front row. The only three boys in the class were way in the back, next to one another.

Alice put her mat near Sophie's and said, "This is a lot better than volleyball."

"How do you know? We haven't done anything yet," said Sophie.

"Maybe we'll get to take a nap," said Alice. "Like kindergarten."

Their giggles were cut off when Ms. Bell spoke again. "I want you to take off your shoes and make yourselves comfortable while everyone gets settled," she said. "Cross your legs and sit quietly. Close your eyes and just relax."

No one ever let them take off their shoes in school. Or told them to relax, for that matter. It was usually the opposite: *Hurry up and do your work. Be quiet and open your books.* Sophie dutifully took off her shoes, sat cross-legged, and closed her eyes.

At first, it felt strange to sit in a room with her eyes closed when she was surrounded by kids she knew. Sophie peeked a few times to see whether anyone was fooling around, but they were all sitting quietly. She finally closed her eyes and kept them closed.

When the sound of the kids in the hall on their way to the cafeteria suddenly dropped away, Sophie opened her eyes again. Ms. Bell had closed the gym doors and was putting a CD into her player. Soft music started to play, one clear flute note at a time.

Sophie closed her eyes again. The gym was unnaturally quiet. It became easier and easier to sit still. Then Ms. Bell spoke.

"Okay, you can open your eyes now." She was sitting with her legs crossed on her own mat in front of them. "I'm happy to see so many of you here. Yoga is the best kind of exercise. It's fun and relaxing, but it will also make you strong." She smiled around at everyone. "Best of all, in yoga everyone gets to move at his or her own pace. It's not a competition. It's you against yourself, doing as much as you can."

That sounded good. Sophie got tired of the way kids in the fourth grade tried to be the best all the time. The best at math, the best at writing, the best at sports.

"By learning the different poses and practicing them at home, every one of you can become stronger. Your body will become leaner," Ms. Bell went on. "If you keep doing yoga, you'll become more coordinated, too, and have more energy. But first, I want to talk about how to breathe."

"How to breathe"? If they didn't know how to do that, they'd be dead. Sophie and Alice looked at each other and giggled. So did some of the other kids.

"I know—it sounds funny," Ms. Bell said, "but bear with me."

She told them to sit up straight and rest their hands on their knees with their palms up. "Now, close your eyes again," she said, "and slowly breathe in and out. You inhale, or breathe in, through your nose. When you exhale, or breathe out, it should be through your mouth."

Sophie closed her eyes and tried to concentrate.

"Inhale . . . and exhale . . ." Ms. Bell's voice was slow and gentle. "When you inhale, feel the air fill your lungs . . . As you breathe, *feel* your body . . . Pay *attention* to your body."

"*Your body.*" There it was again.

Sophie didn't know why it should suddenly feel so embarrassing. Before yesterday, *body* was only a word. Now it felt full of meaning.

She opened an eye to find Alice looking at her, and quickly closed it.

"You're doing great. Let's move on," Ms. Bell said. "Next, I want to teach you some of the yoga poses we're going to use."

Most of the poses were named for animals or things in nature. They learned the cow pose and then the cat pose. Kneeling on their hands and knees, they arched their backs.

"Like Halloween cats," Ms. Bell said. "Stretch your back as high as you can. Feel the stretch. Good."

In the downward dog pose, they had to put their hands and feet flat on the floor and raise their bottoms in the air as high as they could.

"Stretch! That's right," Ms. Bell called. "Try to keep your heels on the floor and *lift* your bottom! Feel the muscles in the backs of your legs!"

Alice looked so funny with her bottom sticking up. Sophie started to laugh. Alice did too, and fell over.

They learned the tree pose next. It was meant to improve their balance. Sophie stood with her arms out to the sides, the way Ms. Bell told them, and rested the sole of her right foot against her left leg. She glanced to see how other kids were doing and saw Destiny put her foot on the floor to steady herself. Sophie started to wobble too. She looked back at the floor and stared as hard as she could at the blue circle in front of her. *Don't fall, don't fall, don't fall,* she told herself.

Slowly, her leg got steadier. Sophie was amazed. By using her brain and concentrating, she was able to calm her body down enough so that she could stand on one leg, still as a tree. She even felt like a tree, except without branches. Maybe she was going to be good at this. She was pretty sure she could already feel herself developing self-control. But then Ms. Bell called, "Do *not* watch your friends! If they wobble, so will you!" So, of course, Sophie had to look at Alice.

That was all it took for the two trees to wobble, giggle, and fall.

FIVE

"It was pretty hard, but it was fun," Alice told Jenna when the other two joined her in line in the cafeteria.

"I think it gets easier when you get stronger," said Sophie.

"Did Alice tell you about my meeting?" It was Destiny. She and Hailey stood holding their trays. "One of my friends is going to tell me about the movie after they watch it," Destiny said.

"You should be there," Hailey said, "unless you're too babyish to hear about the facts of life." She twisted her fists in her eyes and said, "Wah-wah," like a baby.

Destiny laughed.

"I already know about them," Sophie said. "My parents always say, 'Sorry, but it's a fact of life,' when they make us do something we don't want to."

"Mine, too," said Jenna. "Like mold's really going to grow on my teeth if I don't brush them every week."

"Not *that* kind of fact," Hailey said scornfully.

"I think they mean the birds and the bees," said Alice.

"Why don't you just come out and say it?" said Destiny. *"S-E-X."*

Sophie's and Jenna's eyebrows rose up without their even trying. Alice blushed.

"I didn't think so." Destiny and Hailey exchanged superior smiles. "At least *you* might be mature enough to come, Alice," Destiny said.

No way. Sophie wasn't about to let Destiny steal Alice right in front of them. "Alice is coming to *my* meeting," Sophie said.

"I *am*?" said Alice.

"She *is*?" said Jenna.

"You're having a meeting?" Destiny said.

"I don't believe it," said Hailey.

"Well, my mother's a nurse, in case you didn't know," Sophie said. "If I want to know about . . . things . . . I can just ask her."

It wasn't a total lie. Sophie *could* ask her mother.

She never had, because she didn't want to know. It was coming soon enough. Why rush it? She had certainly overheard her mother and Nora talking about girl things. When Nora's voice dropped and she told Mrs. Hartley that she needed to talk to her "in private," Sophie blocked it out. Even so, she'd heard Nora say "that time of the month" often enough, usually when she didn't want to take gym, to know it *meant* something.

Something Sophie didn't want to know about.

"Oh. Well." Hailey looked at Destiny, as usual.

"Fine. Have your three-person meeting," said Destiny. "I already invited all of the other girls to mine. Come on, Hailey."

"Are you crazy?" Jenna said when the girls walked away. "Are you really having a meeting?"

"Destiny will never stop bugging us unless I do," said Sophie.

"I forgot about your mom," Alice said eagerly. "She can tell you everything and you can tell us."

"This is all your fault, Alice," Jenna said as they put their trays on a table and sat down. "I don't know why you're making such a big deal about a dumb movie."

"There's nothing wrong with wanting to know about these things," said Alice.

"There is if you're only doing it because girls like Destiny are pushing you," said Sophie.

"Anything Destiny knows, I don't want to hear," Jenna said. "As far as I'm concerned ..." She pinched her nose shut and raised her eyebrows.

"Me, too," said Sophie. She did the same.

"Me, too." Alice pinched her nose shut, unpinching it long enough to quickly add, "I still think it's okay to know," before she pinched it again.

"I don't see why you won't let me," Nora was saying when Sophie opened the door to the mudroom after school.

"Hair straightening is expensive," Mrs. Hartley said. "Your hair is lovely. You should be proud of it."

"I'll pay for it myself."

Mrs. Hartley and John were sitting at the kitchen table. Mrs. Hartley was having a cup of coffee. Next to her, John was building a pyramid out of his cookies.

Nora paced up and down in front of them.

"No, because if I let you do that, then you'll want me to pay for the *next* thing you have to have, Nora," Mrs. Hartley said patiently. "The list of things you have to have is never-ending."

"Then I'll buy a kit and do it myself," Nora said.

"If you do that, you stand a good chance of damaging your hair."

"You could play soccer with Nora's hair," John said.

"See?" Nora cried. "Even my seven-year-old brother knows how ridiculous it looks."

"John . . ." Mrs. Hartley sighed.

Sophie took the milk out of the refrigerator and poured herself a glass. She lifted the lid of the cookie jar as quietly as she could, the way they'd all perfected so their mother wouldn't hear them getting cookies when they weren't supposed to be eating them, but she wasn't quiet enough.

Nora wheeled around and glared at her. "And don't you say a word."

"Sophie hasn't opened her mouth," said Mrs. Hartley.

"Yes, but I know what she's thinking." Nora

tilted her head to one side and said in a silly, cheerful voice, "'I have curly hair too, and I love it!'"

She sounded exactly like Sophie. Sophie vowed never to try to cheer Nora up, ever again. About anything.

"The only people who say curly hair is wonderful are girls with straight hair, and mothers," Nora said bitterly as she gathered up her books and purse. "I can hardly wait until you get to middle school, Sophie. You're going to *hate* your hair."

"That sounds like something to look forward to," Mr. Hartley said as he came into the kitchen.

"Nobody in this family understands me!" Nora yelled. She rushed past him and pounded up the stairs.

"The stairs in this house sure get a workout," Mr. Hartley commented cheerfully as he looked around the kitchen. "What's for dinner?"

That was Sophie's cue to get out, fast.

Thad was late. Mrs. Hartley had a strict rule about the family eating together during the week. Considering how annoying her mother seemed to find her family, Sophie thought as the rest of them sat down, Mrs. Hartley might have more fun if they ate in front of the TV like other people.

Thad crashed through the mudroom door a minute later, threw his things onto a bench, and slid into a chair. "Glad you could join us," said Mr. Hartley.

"Sorry." Thad speared two pieces of chicken from the plate in the middle of the table with his fork. "Emily's car got a flat tire."

"Why didn't she have her butler change it?" said Nora.

"Nora?"

Nora looked at her father, then down at her plate.

When the phone rang, Nora and Thad both started to get up. Mrs. Hartley said, "*I* will get it," in a firm voice, so they sat back down. Their mother took the phone and went out of the room.

"I thought we weren't allowed to talk on the phone during dinner," Sophie said. No one responded, so she heaved a heavy sigh and kept eating.

Mrs. Hartley carried on a long conversation in the hall in what sounded like somber tones. Dinner was almost over by the time she finally came back into the kitchen. She was smiling.

"Who was that?" Mr. Hartley asked.

"Carol Dashefsky, our assistant director," Mrs. Hartley said cheerfully. "She's sick."

"If she's sick, then why are you so happy?" said Sophie.

"Because it means she can't go to the home health care conference in Chicago next week." Mrs. Hartley sat down and spread her napkin on her lap with exaggerated care. "So I'm going in her place."

"Good for you," said Mr. Hartley.

"Make sure you bring me the little bags of pretzels from the plane," said John.

"Pretzels, shmetzels. Mom will be lucky if they give her a paper napkin on the plane," said Thad. "She'd have better luck robbing the refrigerator in her hotel room."

"For how long?" Nora asked.

"I'll leave on Sunday morning and be gone until next Saturday." Their mother was positively beaming now. She'd gone from wanting to give them away to looking as if she were thrilled to see them.

It's only because she knows she's leaving us, Sophie thought darkly. *Us, her horrible children.*

"What about us?" Sophie said.

"Your father will be here."

Everyone looked at Mr. Hartley, who smiled and waved.

"Dad?" Sophie said doubtfully. "For a whole week?"

"Yes!" Thad pumped the air with his fist. "Dad, for a whole week!"

"No baths! No baths! No baths!" John chanted.

"Listen, Dad," Thad said, leaning toward his father. "Since *she's* not going to be here and you can't drive, how about if I take the car to school?"

Mrs. Hartley usually hated it when they referred to her as "she" even though she was right there. Now she only laughed.

"And so it begins, Tom," she said to Mr. Hartley. "Come on, everyone." She stood up, picked up her glass and plate, and headed for the dishwasher. "Someone get Maura ready for bed. You might as well start practicing. Pretend I'm not here."

Nora grabbed her plate and glass and sidled up to her mother. Sophie was right behind her. "Mom, do you really think this is fair?" Nora whispered furiously.

"Dad's *never* taken care of us for a week," said Sophie.

"You'll be fine." Their mother dismissed their concerns with what Sophie thought was alarming ease. "What Dad doesn't know, he'll figure out."

"How can you be so sure?" Nora hissed.

Mrs. Hartley smiled. "He found the mayonnaise by himself, didn't he?"

Their mother hogged the computer in the family room for almost an hour, making plane and hotel reservations. After that, she went upstairs and laid out her dresses, skirts, and pants on the bed so she could look at them.

"What if Dad's foot gets worse?" Sophie said, watching her from her doorway.

"He's a big boy. He knows how to call the doctor."

"He could get gangrene, you know. If people get gangrene, their limbs have to be cut off."

Mrs. Hartley gave Sophie a measured look and

went back to pulling sweaters and blouses out of her dresser to match them up with the pants and skirts.

"You and Dad better not be getting a divorce," Sophie said after a few minutes. It seemed as if everyone's parents were getting divorced these days. Sophie didn't understand why people got married if they were only going to get divorced. And why didn't the children get a vote?

Sophie would never forgive her parents if they got divorced.

"Oh, Sophie, please." Her mother held a navy blue skirt up to her waist and then a black one. "Which of these looks better?"

"They both look the same."

Her mother held a few more pieces of clothing in front of her and regarded them from different angles in her full-length mirror.

"You act like you're going on vacation," Sophie said.

"What do you want, Sophie?" her mother said absently. "You can see I'm busy."

"I have to talk to you about something."

"Talk to your father."

"I can't talk to him about this."

"Why not?" Mrs. Hartley knelt in front of the closet and yanked out a pair of shoes, tossing them onto the floor as if she'd rather hurl them at someone. "Why is it always the *mother* that children have to whine to about needing *this,* and not wanting to do *that,* and why can't they do *such and such*?" Her mother hurled another pair. "Where is the *father* when all of these earthshattering conversations are taking place?"

"You're going to ruin those if you keep throwing them," said Sophie.

"Go away!" her mother said. She waved her hand at Sophie without turning around. "Go and talk to your father! I'm off-duty until next weekend. Besides, your father needs the practice."

"'Go *away*'?" Sophie said incredulously. "'Go away,' when I need to talk to you about something important? Fine!" Sophie thought about shutting the door very loudly as she left the room. Then she realized her mother wouldn't even notice and fell into an even worse mood.

There was a cloud of steam at the other end of

the hall. Nora had opened the bathroom door after taking her shower. Her showers lasted so long these days that the bathroom looked like a sauna when she was finished.

Part of Sophie wanted to say something about its being Nora's fault their mother was so happy to leave them. The other part needed someone to talk to.

"Mom's being rude," Sophie said, leaning against the bathroom doorway as Nora brushed her teeth. "She acts like she's going on vacation."

"Let's face it." Nora spat out toothpaste and smiled at herself in the mirror, checking for food between her teeth. "She's running away from home."

"Really?"

Nora shrugged. "You have to admit, she seems pretty happy."

"She must really hate us," Sophie said glumly.

"Oh, Sophie, please. You always exaggerate." Nora put her toothbrush into the bathroom cabinet and closed it. "She wants a break, that's all. And someone else is paying for her hotel. What's not to be happy about?"

When it was time for bed, Sophie went downstairs to say good night to her parents. She had decided that if her mother apologized for being rude, Sophie would relent and talk to her about the movie. After all, she really needed to know.

When she got to the bottom of the stairs, she heard her parents talking in the kitchen. It sounded friendly. Good. It was safe to go in.

"I'm making a list of things you need to know while I'm gone," Sophie heard her mother saying as she got close. "Irene Dubowski will take Maura to daycare and bring her home."

"Irene Dubowski . . ." said her dad. "Isn't she that young, good-looking gal you and I ran into at the mall?"

"Tom!" Mrs. Hartley snapped.

"What? All I said is that she's nice-looking."

Sophie turned to head back up the stairs.

Sometimes her dad sounded as clueless as Thad, Sophie thought as she went back into her room. Now what was she going to do?

There was only one solution.

Nora's book.

Sophie was going to have to sneak up to Nora's

room, which was strictly off-limits to her, find the dumb book, and look for something she could tell Alice. If Nora discovered Sophie and strangled her, well, their mother would just have to feel guilty for the rest of her life. It would serve her right. Sophie was sick of the whole thing.

She stood in front of her mirror and willed herself to become a tree.

SIX

"Sophie!" Megan Parsley hurried up to Sophie when she came out of the girls' room the next day, with Caroline Vega and Gabriella Klein behind her. "Can we come to your meeting?" Megan said breathlessly.

"Alice told us," Caroline said. "Destiny invited us to hers, but we'd much rather go to yours."

"Destiny's so mean," Gabriella added. "Please?"

Two more fourth-grade girls stopped Sophie on her way back to class. Sophie marched into Mrs. Stearns's room and stood in front of Alice's desk. Alice buried her head deeper in the book she was reading.

"How could you?" Sophie said.

"What happened?" said Jenna.

Sophie told her.

"Good going, Alice," Jenna said.

"I couldn't help it," Alice said. "Destiny's trying

to boss girls into going to her meeting, but a lot of them are afraid of her."

"Well, there's a problem," Sophie said, and told them about Chicago.

"What are you going to do?" Alice's face went white. "I know! Nora can tell you."

"Are you kidding?" said Jenna. "Nora never tells Sophie anything."

"She has a book," Sophie admitted reluctantly. "My mother gave it to her a few years ago. I'm pretty sure it's about P-U. Nora said it was about *girl business* and wouldn't let me look at it."

"That must be it," Alice said. "My mother left a book on my bed one time and told me it was about love and marriage, but I was too embarrassed to look at it. I don't understand what those things have to do with P-U, do you?"

"Don't ask me," Jenna said.

"Nora probably won't lend it to me," Sophie said, "but I'm sure it's somewhere in her room."

"You can find it. You know how sneaky you are," Alice said.

"Yeah, creep up to Nora's room and look through her stuff like the good old days," Jenna said. "Just make sure you bring a parachute in case she starts coming up the stairs and you have to jump."

"Please?" Alice said.

"Oh, all right!" Sophie sat at her desk. "But I'm not going to sit there and read the whole book. You have to promise you'll let it go after I tell you a few things."

"I promise," Alice said. "Thank you, Sophie."

"And don't tell anyone else!"

"I won't."

Unfortunately, Alice had already told four more girls.

Mr. Hartley and Thad drove Mrs. Hartley to the airport on Sunday morning. Nora had said goodbye the night before so she could sleep in. Sophie waved goodbye as they pulled out of the driveway and went back into the house. She heard John shouting in the family room.

"Back off!" he shouted as Sophie went down the hall.

Then, "Back off!" a little voice echoed.

"Mom's going to kill you, John," Sophie said. She leaned against the doorway and crossed her arms.

John was standing in front of Maura wearing his white tiger uniform. He had his feet planted wide apart and his hands poised in front of him like the lethal weapons he said they were. Maura looked like a miniature mirror image, except her pajamas were covered with clowns.

"Back off!" John yelled again. He chopped the air a few times.

"Back off!" Maura repeated. She waved her arms around as if she were swimming.

"Wait until the next time Mom asks Maura to do something and Maura shouts, 'Back off!'" Sophie told him. "Why can't you teach her to say something helpful, like 'Can I please clean Sophie's room?'"

"That's way too long for her," said John.

There was the sound of footsteps pounding down the stairs. Nora rushed into the room, clutching the phone.

"Where's Mom?" Nora cried. She looked

around frantically, as if Mrs. Hartley might have ducked behind the couch.

"She's gone," said Sophie. "Dad and Thad took her to the airport."

"Omigod," Nora said. "How could she?"

"Don't tell me you already miss her."

"Don't be an idiot."

"Then what's wrong?"

Nora sank onto the couch. "I've been invited to a party on Friday night, that's what's wrong," she said.

"I thought you liked going to parties."

"You don't know anything, do you?"

Sophie recognized all the signs. If she wasn't careful, in another second Nora was going to end up blaming Sophie for whatever was wrong. "So," Sophie said cautiously, "you aren't happy because . . . ?"

"Because Ian's going to pick me up, that's why," Nora said impatiently. "Well, Ian's mother."

"Isn't that good?" Sophie said. "You like Ian."

Nora stood up and paced back and forth. "Good, that the first boy to pick me up for a party, ever, is going to do it when only my corny father, my obnoxious older brother, and my nutso younger brother are going to be here?"

"What good would it do if Mom were here?"

"She'd make Dad behave, for one thing," said Nora. "And she'd make Thad go out for the night, and maybe plan for John to be taking a bath so he doesn't try to karate-chop Ian."

"Back off, Ian!" John shouted, chopping the corner of the coffee table.

"See what I mean?" Nora sank onto the couch again.

"I still don't see why it's such a big deal," Sophie said.

"Can't you see Dad?" Nora sounded desperate. "Cracking jokes and thinking he's being funny? And Thad . . . ?" Nora moaned and buried her head in her hands. "It'll be the perfect chance for him to embarrass me in front of a boy."

Put like that, it did sound dangerous.

"Maybe they won't be like that," said Sophie. "If you talk to Dad before Ian gets here, he won't crack jokes. And he'll make Thad and John behave."

"How? They're boys."

"Speaking of them . . ."

There was the sudden sound of voices in the kitchen. Mr. Hartley and Thad were home. John ran into the hall and assumed his combat stance.

"Men rule!" he shouted. "We have more men in our family than girls for a whole week!"

"Cool it, John." Thad came into the room, gave John's head a quick noogie, then fell into a chair and started checking the messages on his phone.

"What are you talking about, John?" said Nora. "It's three and three."

"We have Maura," Sophie agreed.

"Maura doesn't count," John said. "She's only a baby."

"What did you have planned—family hand-to-hand combat?" said Nora.

"She dumped me." Thad said suddenly, staring at his phone in disbelief. "I can't believe it. The girl dumped me."

"Who?" Sophie asked.

"Who do you think? Emily," Nora told her. Then, to Thad: "Did she say why?"

"Emily dumped him in a *text message?*" said Sophie.

"She met a guy who's on the debate team at East," Thad said. "East! I can't believe it."

East was the other high school in town. Thad went to West. There was a fierce rivalry between the two. "We beat those losers every year in football and soccer," Thad said. "I can't believe a girl would choose a debate-team wimp over an athlete."

"It's an outrage," said Nora.

Thad shot her a look. "Girls," he said disgustedly. He stood up and shoved his phone into his pocket. "Come on, John. Let's go to the garage and lift some weights."

"Yeah. *Girls*," John echoed.

"Where are you two going?" Sophie heard their dad ask.

"To where there are no girls," said John.

"See what I mean?" Nora said. "And you think Dad can change anything?"

"Well, we got Mom there in plenty of time," Mr. Hartley reported proudly as he came into the family room. "This break is going to be good for her. She started having last-minute jitters in the car, but I told her to relax." He rubbed his hands together and smiled. "What could go wrong in a week?"

Sophie and Nora looked back at him.

"What?" Mr. Hartley's smile faded as he saw their faces. "Did something happen while I was gone?"

"Help," Nora bleated as she fell over sideways on the couch. "When's Mom coming home?"

On Monday at lunchtime, Sophie told Jenna and Alice about Thad and Emily.

"That's nothing," Jenna said. "One time, my brother Sam broke up with a girl he took to a party by texting her from the bathroom."

"I'm telling you right now," Sophie said. "I'm not having anything to do with the boy-girl thing when I get older."

"I think you have to," said Alice. "Everyone has to go through that stuff."

"Don't start that again," said Jenna.

"What's Destiny doing?" said Sophie.

They all looked over at the next table. With Hailey trailing her, Destiny was walking behind the row of seated girls, handing out slips of hot-pink paper. "One for you . . . and one for you . . ." Destiny reached the end of the table and crossed to where Sophie, Alice, and Jenna were seated.

"And one for you, *Alice,* in case you change your mind," Destiny said. She put a slip in front of Alice and gave a little pinch to the shoulder of Alice's T-shirt. "I love your tie-dyeing. So cute."

"What is it?" Sophie asked after Destiny moved on.

"I don't know," said Alice.

"Try reading it," Jenna said.

Alice blushed furiously as she read it. "It's just something dumb," she said.

"We knew that," said Sophie, "but what?"

"A reminder about her meeting on Friday."

"What an idiot," Jenna said. "She knows you're going to Sophie's."

"I know." Alice hurriedly stuffed the note into her lunch bag.

"So why aren't you tearing it up?" said Sophie.

"Destiny might be insulted."

"Who cares?" said Jenna. "Tear it into tiny pieces and throw them in the air like confetti. That'll show her."

"I'll get in trouble with the lunch monitor if I do that," Alice said. She reluctantly pulled out the paper and looked at it. "I'm supposed to RSVP," she said miserably.

"Yeah, right," said Jenna.

Sophie looked at Alice without saying anything. Under Sophie's watchful eye, Alice slowly stood up and went to throw the paper into the garbage.

"Come on, Alice," Sophie said when Alice got back. "We'll feel better after we do yoga."

Destiny and Hailey passed them in the hall. "By the way," Destiny said to Alice, "I saw what you did with my note. I didn't mean it about your T-shirt. Tie-dyeing is so nerdy."

"Wah-wah," said Hailey.

"I hate Destiny," Alice said as Destiny and Hailey disappeared through the gym's double doors.

"I thought you weren't supposed to say you hate anyone," said Jenna.

"When it's girls like Destiny, who are mean to people for no reason, she can," Sophie said. She put her arm around Alice's shoulders. "She's just jealous because you and me and Jenna are best friends. Let's go be trees."

Sophie got on the computer as soon as she got home so she could finish her homework before

Nora arrived. That way, while Nora was glued to the computer doing hers, Sophie could sneak up to her room and find the book.

The trouble was that Nora arrived home soon after Sophie. "Hurry up on that thing," Nora said as she came into the room.

The Hartleys kept their computer in the family room. Thad had saved enough money from his summer job to buy himself a laptop, but Nora and Sophie had to share. John played games on it only on the weekends.

Even with only two of them using the computer, they usually bickered over whose turn it was. Mrs. Hartley had gotten so sick of it, she'd said she was going to put up a time sheet if she heard one more argument about it.

Nora and Sophie had resorted to arguing in whispers. They kept their voices low now, just to be safe.

"Not yet," Sophie whispered. "I've only been on it for ten minutes."

"So?" Nora hissed. "I have an important report to write."

"I have important homework, too, Nora."

"Take it from me: Nothing is that important in fourth grade."

"It is too!"

"You're such a brat," Nora said.

"I am not."

"You are too."

Their voices had risen without their realizing it.

"I'm too old to be a brat," said Sophie.

Nora snorted. "What does age have to do with it?"

"Only babies and little kids are called brats. Ten is too old."

"Too old? Are you joking? You don't know what you're talking about."

"Oh, I don't?" Sophie said. She quickly typed "brat" on the computer. "See?" she said, pointing to the definition that appeared on the screen. "'Brat: an ill-mannered, annoying child.'" She sat up straight. "I am *not* a child."

"You're not a child? Who are you kidding?" Nora peered furiously over Sophie's shoulder and jabbed at the screen. "What about this one, then?

The second definition. 'An ill-mannered, imma-ture person'!" Nora read triumphantly. "That's you, Sophie."

"I am not immature!" Sophie yelled.

"Oh, dear. Little Miss Sunshine's losing her temper."

"And stop calling me that! I'm sick of it! It's *you* who's immature. You're a bigger brat than I am, too!"

"Oh, that was a mature thing to say."

"I hate you sometimes, Nora."

"Well, I hate you all the time, Sophie."

"Excuse me."

Mr. Hartley was standing in the doorway with an apron over his sweatshirt and an amazed look on his face. "What are you two doing?" he asked.

Nora and Sophie looked at each other and then back at their father.

"We're having a conversation," Nora said.

"We're talking," said Sophie.

"No." Mr. Hartley advanced into the room. "That was not a conversation. That was not talking. What that was was arguing—very loudly, and in a very immature way—about which one of you was more immature."

Nora and Sophie glanced at each other again.

"Is this how you always talk to each other?" Mr. Hartley asked.

"Well, yeah," said Nora.

"Most of the time," Sophie said.

"No wonder your mother's so irritable these days," their dad said. "Listening to you two is enough to make anybody irritable."

Sophie and Nora were oddly united. If they had been confronted by their mother, each of them would have rushed to put the blame on the other one. They didn't dare try that with Mr. Hartley.

"If I hear one more word about whose turn it is on that thing," he said, "I'm going to pull the plug for the rest of the week. You can find a quill and some ink and do your homework the old-fashioned way."

Sophie and Nora remained in an uneasy silence after he left the room.

"The rest of the week"?

Their dad had definitely sounded like he meant it.

"I'll be off in twenty minutes," Sophie whispered.

"You'd better be," Nora whispered back. She picked up her books. "Heaven help us," she sighed. "When's Mom coming home?"

SEVEN

Sophie almost chickened out. Even putting her hand on the knob of the door to the attic stairs felt dangerous. If Nora caught her, she was dead meat.

Clutching the pile of laundry that someone had left on the stairs below and Sophie had swooped up so that in the event Nora caught her, she could tell Nora she was putting away clean clothes, Sophie opened the door and started up the steps. They didn't have carpeting, so she had to tread softly. When a step creaked, Sophie stopped and listened. There wasn't a sound. She hurried the rest of the way to the top, before she could lose her nerve.

Good. Both doors—the door to Nora's room and the door to the storage room across the hall—were open. Sophie was pretty sure she couldn't be legally charged with trespassing if Nora's door was open. If it came to that. Calling the police, that is.

Sophie shook herself. She was being dramatic. It was only because their dad was so mad at them. If Nora caught her and they got into another fight, all heck would break loose. There was no telling what Mr. Hartley would do, and Sophie didn't want to find out.

She tiptoed into Nora's room, went over to the bookshelf, and scanned the titles. *Body, body, body* . . . Nope. Nothing. Where would Nora have hidden it? Sophie looked around the room.

Aha—under the bed! As Sophie crouched to look, the same stair that had creaked before cried out. She leaped to her feet and spun around as Nora appeared at the top of the stairs.

"What are you doing up here?" Nora said furiously. Thankfully, she whispered it. She obviously didn't want to get into more trouble with their dad, either.

"I thought you were on the computer!" Sophie whispered back.

"I forgot my notes!"

"I'm helping Dad by putting away clothes," Sophie whispered. "I thought these were yours."

"Yeah, right. Like I'm wearing Maura's pajamas

these days," Nora hissed, plucking at the clown material in the middle of the pile.

"I mean, I'm supposed to put them in the footlocker in the storage room. Maura's too big for them."

"The storage room is over there," Nora said in a deadly quiet voice. She pointed.

"I know where the storage room is," Sophie said with as much dignity as she could muster.

"Omigod!" Nora slapped her hands over her face. "You're wearing shoes!"

Nora was right. In her haste to find the book, Sophie had ignored both Nora's ironclad rule about no shoes *and* the basket Nora had left at the bottom of the stairs where visitors were meant to leave theirs. Sophie saw the long black marks from her rubber soles on the white floor near the door and picked up speed.

"Shhh, I'm going. Don't yell. Remember Dad." She scurried into the storage room across the hall and dumped the clothes on the floor as Nora watched. Slipping off her shoes, Sophie waved them in the air. "Happy now?" she said, and escaped quickly down the steps.

"If you scratched the stairs, I'm going to kill you!" Nora hissed after her. She must have spotted the scuff mark on her floor, because Sophie heard a gasp, followed by a stifled shriek.

Sophie ran as fast as she could on tiptoe down the hall and into her room. She closed the door and leaned with her back against it for a moment before leaping across the room to lie on her bed and rest her head on Patsy's stomach.

Patsy's comforting purr reminded her of the "Om" they'd listened to on a CD at the end of yoga. Sophie lay still, feeling her heart slow down, until Patsy struggled to get out from under the weight of Sophie's head. Then Sophie moved over and stared at the ceiling.

All of this near-death-by-sister drama because of a movie.

A dumb movie, a movie that embarrassed everyone before anyone had even seen it. And now she, Sophie, was holding a meeting about it when she still didn't know anything.

Why did P-U-berty feel so embarrassing? Even thinking about saying it that way didn't help much anymore. Maybe if she said it three times fast.

Puberty, puberty, puberty.

Yuck.

"Good going, Dad." Thad sniffed appreciatively as he came into the kitchen after practice. "That smells like something we can actually eat."

Mr. Hartley had taken his meat loaf out of the oven. Now he was taking out the baked potatoes, one by one, wearing Mrs. Hartley's flowered oven mitts. "I used your mother's recipe," he said. "Since John set the table and the girls got the rest of it ready, you can take cleanup."

"Yeah, okay." Thad turned on the tap to wash his hands. "How's your foot? You're not limping anymore."

"Much better," Mr. Hartley said. "I'm beginning to think Mom planned the whole thing so she'd be free to go to Chicago."

Maura was sitting on the floor, patting Patsy. At the mention of Mrs. Hartley, she took her thumb out of her mouth and said, "Mommy?"

"Mommy will be home soon," Nora told her. "I hope."

Mr. Hartley had kept Maura home from daycare

for the afternoon and let her play with pieces of wood in the sawdust while he'd cleaned up his workshop. She had the happy, slightly dazed look of a toddler who could easily fall asleep sitting up.

When John had arrived home from school, he'd complained it was no fair that Maura had gotten to stay home for part of the day and he hadn't, so Mr. Hartley had promised he'd give him a surprise after dinner. John was seated at the table now, systematically biting off the ends of the french fries on his plate before lining them up in a neat row.

"It would be nice if you waited for the rest of us, John," said Mr. Hartley. He lifted Maura into her highchair as Sophie put a glass of milk at each place. Nora finished tossing the salad and put it in the middle of the table.

"I have to put my spit on them or Thad will steal them," John said.

"Nice, Thad," Mr. Hartley said as he sat down.

"I'm teaching him important survival skills, right, John?" Thad said. "That's what older brothers are for."

"I thought they were to annoy their younger sister," Nora said.

"I'm glad you said that, Nora," Mr. Hartley said pleasantly as he picked up his fork. "I thought we'd try something new in the way of conversation tonight."

Uh-oh. Sophie and Nora looked at each other. This had to have something to do with them.

"In the interest of family harmony," Mr. Hartley went on, "and also out of respect for your mother, we're going to practice talking pleasantly to one another for the entire meal."

"'Pleasantly'?" Nora said.

"All the way through dessert?" said Sophie.

"What does Mom have to do with it?" said Thad.

"You guys are wearing her down, Thad," Mr. Hartley said. "The way you talk to one another is ridiculous. You snipe at one another, you insult one another . . . I haven't heard one of you say something nice or supportive to another since I got home."

"But . . ." Sophie started.

"No buts, Sophie. And it's no good trying to blame the other guy," Mr. Hartley said. "You're all guilty."

Sophie slowly closed her mouth.

"Nice try, LMS," Nora said under her breath.

"That's exactly what I mean, Nora."

Nora looked down at her plate.

"No wonder your mother is worn out," Mr. Hartley said. "I would be too if I had to listen to you all the time."

It was weird, hearing their dad talk like this. He was saying what their mother always said, but it sounded different when he said it. Everybody was not only listening to him, but *hearing* him—Sophie could tell. Nora and Thad weren't jumping in and saying something sarcastic, the way they normally would have.

"So here's the deal," their dad said. "From now on, if you don't have something nice to say, don't say anything."

Nothing but nice? That could lead to a very quiet dinner.

"Only tonight, right?" Nora said. "You can't mean forever."

"Let's see how it goes," said Mr. Hartley. He sounded a lot more cheerful about the idea than everybody else at the table looked. "Not bad, if I do say so myself," he said, eating a bite of meat loaf.

They silently watched him chew. Mr. Hartley took another bite and smiled. When it looked as if no one else was going to say anything, Sophie said, "It's delicious, Dad."

She didn't care if Nora glared at her. It *was* delicious. Besides, it was the only nice thing Sophie could think of to say. Every time she started to think, all that came into her mind was how on earth she was going to steal Nora's book without getting killed. Now it was someone else's turn.

Sophie glanced around the table. She could practically hear the gears in everyone's brain working. Dinner was starting to feel like third-grade Spanish. Ms. Brioso had come to their classroom twice a week. She'd taught them how to count and say things such as "Hello" and "How are you?" and "My name is . . ."

One day she announced they were going to speak Spanish for the entire lesson. No English. Ms. Brioso said she would start.

"*Hola,*" she'd said. "*¿Cómo está usted?*"

There was a long silence. Kids looked around

uneasily, hoping someone else was going to answer. Finally, a voice said, *"Bueno."*

Another silence. Then another voice: *"Bueno, bueno."*

When a third voice said, *"Bueno, bueno, bueno,"* and all of the kids started to laugh, they went back to speaking English.

Now Thad was the first one to break the silence at the table.

"Did you speak to Mom today?" he said.

"I did," said Mr. Hartley. "She said she's having a good time but that she's doing a lot of sitting around, listening to people say the same things over and over again."

"It sounds like school," said Nora. "That's not negative about anyone in the family," she added quickly when Mr. Hartley looked at her.

"How was your day, Thad?" said Mr. Hartley.

"Emily dumped me yesterday, so I was bummed for a bit," Thad said.

"Who's Emily?"

Ordinarily, Nora would have said, "Thad's stuck-up girlfriend." Instead, she told her dad, "Thad's girlfriend."

"Ex-girlfriend," Thad said.

"I thought you were going out with someone called Mia," said Mr. Hartley.

"That was last month. What?" Nora protested when Thad looked at her. "I didn't say anything negative. Dad wanted to know who Emily was."

"Well, I'm sorry Emily dumped you," said Mr. Hartley.

"Yeah. It's really inconvenient." Thad shrugged. "Now I have to find someone else to take to a party on Friday night."

"I'm going to a party on Friday night too." Nora's words came out in a rush. "Ian Bishop asked me. His mother's driving us."

"Is this an official date?" her dad said.

"I guess so." Nora sounded surprised and pleased. "His mom's picking up a few other kids on the way, but I'm the only one Ian asked."

"I know Ian Bishop," said Thad.

"You do?" said Nora.

"He was at the soccer camp where I assisted last summer," Thad said. "He plays the sax, right?"

"Right."

"He's a good guy."

"I know! Isn't he great?"

Sophie couldn't remember the last time Nora had looked or sounded as happy.

"Where's the party and what time does it end?" Mr. Hartley asked.

"You're getting pretty good at this," Sophie told him.

"At Sammy Brown's house," Nora told him. "Mom knows Sammy from our old ballet carpool. Her parents will be there. And it ends at ten o'clock. Ian's mom will bring me home."

"That sounds all right, then." Mr. Hartley polished off his baked potato and put his fork and knife on his plate. "How about you, Sophie? I suppose you have a date for Friday night too?"

"I'm never getting involved with that dumb boy-girl stuff," Sophie said.

"Don't be so sure of that," said Nora.

"I've been learning yoga," Sophie said. "I like it a lot. I'm good at it, too. A person can use their brain to control their whole body."

"Even her mouth?" said Mr. Hartley.

"Wait a minute," Nora said. "Isn't that negative?"

"Not at all," said Mr. Hartley. "I was just commenting on an interesting fact."

"Yeah, right . . ."

"They're talking about having the football team do yoga," said Thad. "Maybe you can show me a few moves."

"They're called poses."

"I have my own news," Mr. Hartley announced. "I invited Mrs. Dubowski to dinner Thursday night."

The young, good-looking Mrs. Dubowski? thought Sophie. Without their mother home?

"You mean, like a date?" she said.

"No, Sophie, not like a date," said Mr. Hartley. "She dropped Maura off at lunchtime, and we started talking about food because I was fixing dinner. Mrs. Dubowski said she was making stuffed cabbage, so I told her that my mother used to make stuffed cabbage all the time when I was young and that I love it. She said she'd make enough for the whole family and drop it off on Thursday, so I invited her to stay and enjoy it with us."

"I want peanut butter," said John.

"Does Mom know?" said Sophie.

"What's to know?" Nora said, rolling her eyes.

"Relax, Soph," said Thad. "If Mrs. Dubowski tries anything, Dad'll have five chaperones here to protect him."

They all laughed.

"Protect him from what?" said John.

"Nothing, John," said Mr. Hartley. "Your brother's being a wise guy. Eat up."

They finished the meal listening to John tell a long story about how he and Trevor had built a fort in the playground during recess and were having a really fun time playing war, but then this boy Jeffrey came along and tried to knock it down, so Trevor and John had done their tae kwon do on him and they'd all ended up being sent to the principal's office.

"Way to go, defending your territory," said Thad.

"That wasn't so bad, now, was it?" Mr. Hartley asked when dinner was finished. "Wait. Before everyone gets up, I want each of you to say something nice about the meal."

There was a short silence. Then Thad said, "The food was good."

"The food *was* good," said Nora.

"The food was *very* good," said Sophie.

"The food was very, very, very—"

"Okay, John. We get the picture." Mr. Hartley laughed. "I guess I asked for that. You did a fine job, all of you."

"Whew!" Nora said while they were clearing the table. "I don't know if I can take the pressure of too many more dinners like this. I'm exhausted."

"I may have to go a few rounds with the punching bag after being so nice," said Thad. He snatched the last two french fries off John's plate as he stood up.

"Hey, you big bully!" John shouted.

"PICK ON SOMEONE YOUR OWN SIZE!"

Everybody looked at Maura in astonishment.

"Way to go, Maura!" said Thad.

"That's what the mouse says in the book!" Sophie cried. "It worked! I did it! I taught her how to talk!"

"Now tell him to back off!" John coached. "Say, 'Back off!' real loud."

"What's going on?" Mr. Hartley asked as they all clustered around Maura's highchair.

"That's the longest sentence Maura has ever said," Nora told him.

"Wonderful. Just what this family needs," her dad said. "Another talker."

Maura was pleased by all the attention. Thad and John high-fived her a few times, and then Nora lifted her out of her highchair and carried her upstairs to put her to bed. Mr. Hartley took John upstairs to show him his surprise, while Sophie swiped halfheartedly at the table with a sponge and Thad finished loading the dishwasher. When Sophie went into the family room to use the computer, she could hear John shouting and laughing in the bathroom.

"What's John doing?" Sophie asked when Nora came down.

"Dad's letting him brush his teeth in the bathtub," said Nora.

"In the same water that he washed in? That was his surprise?"

"John thinks it's great."

"I wonder how he got to be such a wacko," Sophie said. She stood up. "I'm finished, if you want to use this."

"Good." Nora sat down in front of the computer.

"I think being Mr. Mom is getting to Dad, don't you?" said Sophie. "I mean, having to be nice at dinner and everything."

"Ya think?" Nora said cheerfully. Sophie could tell she was still happy that Thad had said Ian was a good guy and that their dad had called it a date.

"Or, to follow Dad's rule," Nora said. She stopped typing and looked at Sophie. "Maybe I should say, 'My, what an interesting observation, sister dear.'"

"I like that."

"Well, don't get too used to it."

"Hey, Nora." Thad stuck his head in the doorway on his way upstairs. "Tell Ian that if he tries any moves on Friday night, he'll have to answer to me."

"Thad!" Nora cried.

Sophie had never heard her sister sound so happy to say their brother's name.

Luckily, Nora was in the shower later when Mr. Hartley shouted, "Who took the pile of Maura's clean clothes I left on the stairs?" Sophie ran up to the attic in her bare feet and brought them back down.

"I probably shouldn't ask why they were up there," her dad said when she handed them to him.

"Probably not," Sophie said.

"I should probably just be thankful none of you has done away with one of the others, at this point."

"Definitely."

"You know, Sophie," Mr. Hartley said thoughtfully, "there's a lot more to this motherhood business than meets the eye. Don't rush into anything."

"Dad, I'm only ten."

"Right. Right." Her dad turned and walked slowly down the hall. "Well, good night."

EIGHT

On Thursday, the fifth-grade girls filed past Mrs. Stearns's room in the middle of the morning. Mrs. Stearns's class were writing in their journals. The door was open, but there wasn't a sound coming from the hall. Most of the girls walking past were looking straight ahead, as if they were going to something very serious. There was a kind of nervous, hushed feeling in the air.

Sophie looked across the aisle to see if Jenna had noticed them. Jenna pinched her nose, making Sophie giggle.

"How are you two coming with your stories?" Mrs. Stearns called.

"Good." They both hunched over their journals again.

"Did you see them?" Alice said hurriedly when their class lined up for lunch. "How long do you think the movie will last?"

"Who cares?" said Sophie.

They were almost finished eating when the cafeteria doors flew open and the fifth-grade girls came in. They were making much more noise now, giggling and squealing, falling against one another and laughing. They moved toward tables in small packs.

"I can't believe what we have to do," one of them squealed. She whispered something to another girl and they both shrieked.

"It was so embarrassing," said another.

"What's Destiny up to now?" Jenna said as Destiny moved slowly down the table next to theirs, stopping behind each girl to say something and make a mark in her notebook.

"Knowing Destiny, she's checking her RSVPs," Sophie said.

"What if you don't find Nora's book tonight?" Alice asked.

"I will," Sophie said.

She didn't feel at all confident, however. Time was running out. She had to either find the book or ask Nora herself. The idea of Nora's reaction was excruciating, but Sophie was desperate. All she could hope was that Nora would be in a good mood because of her date. That would make it two nights in a row if she was, which was rare, but a miracle might happen.

Sophie really needed a miracle.

A miracle did happen. Two miracles. Well, one thing that made Sophie feel relieved, and one miracle.

The first was that Sophie talked to her mother on the phone.

"Did Dad tell you Mrs. Dubowski's coming to dinner tonight?" Sophie said.

"Yes. That was nice of Dad to invite her," said Mrs. Hartley. "Her husband died when he was very young. She had to raise two children on her own and now she's raising her grandchild."

"Grandchild?" said Sophie. "I thought she was the young, good-looking one."

Mrs. Hartley laughed. "Leave it to your father," she said. "Gina McFarley was the one we ran into at the mall. Mrs. Dubowski is a lovely woman. You'll enjoy her."

"We were joking with Dad about it being a date," Sophie said.

"Tell that to Mrs. Dubowski. She'll get a kick out of it."

The second miracle was that when Nora got home from school, she was in great spirits. After Sophie handed the phone to their father, Nora reported that when she'd told Ian her brother was Thad from soccer camp, Ian had said that Thad was a really great guy.

That was all it had taken. One "really great guy" and Nora was floating on air.

"That means they like each other, so when Ian picks me up, Thad won't try to embarrass me," she told Sophie. "At least, he better not."

"Nora!" Mr. Hartley called from the kitchen. "Mom wants to talk to you."

"It's probably about my date." Nora rolled her eyes, but Sophie could tell she didn't mind. "I'm sure Mom wants to give me all sorts of advice."

Nora came back with the phone pressed to her ear and wandered around the family room as she talked. Sophie worked on the computer and tried to act as if she weren't eavesdropping.

"Dad keeps calling it an *official* date," Nora said. "Like there's an unofficial date."

She seemed to like saying *date*—she'd been repeating it a lot. While Mrs. Hartley answered, Nora walked over to Mr. Hartley's favorite chair to inspect her face in the mirror above it. She smoothed first one eyebrow and then the other with the tip of her finger. "I know . . . I know . . . Did you tell him not to tell any corny jokes?" Nora gathered her hair on top of her head with one hand and smiled at herself in the mirror. She was practicing smiling at Ian. Sophie had watched her do that many times when they'd shared a bedroom.

Nora never smiled like that at anyone in the family. They all would have thought she was sick.

"Good," Nora said. "And I don't have to worry about Thad. He's going on a date too."

There it was again.

Then, "Mom! I already know that."

Sophie looked up, alarmed. Nora sounded more like her old annoyed self. *Please please please,* Sophie pleaded silently. *Don't spoil things, Mom. Not now.*

"Okay. I said I will, and I will." Nora frowned.

Say date, *say* date, Sophie urged. *That'll make Nora happy again.*

"I wish you were too," Nora said. "Except you'd probably want to take pictures and I'd die of embarrassment."

Nora listened for another moment, and then her smile came back and she laughed. "Okay," she said. "I love you, too."

Sophie couldn't remember the last time she'd heard Nora tell their mother she loved her. This wonderful mood couldn't go on much longer.

It was now or never.

When Nora walked past Sophie's room before dinner as Sophie was lying on her bed reading, Sophie called, "Nora?"

She didn't have a clue as to what she was going to say.

There was a short silence and then Nora appeared in her doorway. "What?" she said. She glanced at her watch. "You have exactly ten seconds. I have to go up and try on the skirt I bought for Sammy's party."

Sophie shut her book and sat up. "Do you remember the movie?" she asked.

Nora looked puzzled.

"Some girls say 'the *movie.*'"

Nora's face cleared and she laughed. "Oh, the *movie,*" she drawled, sounding just like Destiny. "Don't tell me they make girls watch that in the fourth grade these days."

"No, it's still the fifth grade," Sophie said. "But the fifth graders saw it today, and now all the fourth-grade girls are dying to know what it's about."

"The lead-up to that thing is so embarrassing." Nora came in slowly and sat on the end of what had been her bed when they'd shared the room. "For a whole year before, everybody dreads it, but it's not so bad when you finally see it. Well, it's kind of weird when you're watching it, but you get over it." She stopped. "You don't want me to tell you about it, do you?"

"Nonononono," said Sophie.

"Whew."

"It's just that there's this girl, Destiny . . ." Sophie told Nora about Destiny's meeting and Alice's invitation and what Destiny had said about the facts of life and being immature. "Now, whenever she and Hailey walk past us, they pretend they're crying like babies."

"She sounds like Lisa Kellogg," Nora said. "In the fifth grade, Lisa went around telling everyone that if she ever got a French poodle, she was going to name it Nora after my hair. She and all of her friends made barking noises when I walked by. I still can't stand her."

"So you understand," Sophie said. Then, sheepishly: "Oh, and it kind of ended up that I'm holding a meeting too."

"You're holding a meeting when you're completely clueless?" Nora said. "I don't know how you get yourself into these things."

"I don't know either," Sophie said. "But there are going to be about ten girls and they'll all be looking at me and I don't know what to tell them. All I need are a few things I can say. Most girls my age don't want to know *every*thing. At least, the girls coming to my meeting don't. They just want to know a tiny bit. Two key words or something. That's all I need."

Thad popped his head in the door and looked interested. "Two key words about what?" he said, with his uncanny older-brother knack of knowing exactly when his sisters didn't want him around.

"Don't say anything," Sophie begged Nora.

"Poor Sophie," Nora told him. "The fifth-grade girls went to see that movie today that we were all forced to watch. Don't you remember? The one about 'the beauty of human development,' as they called it." Nora snorted. "Who do they think they're kidding?"

"Yeah. They should come right out and call it *The Weird and Bizarre Things Your Body Is About to Go Through but Nobody Wants to Talk About*," Thad said. "Then kids could laugh about it."

"I'm so embarrassed." Sophie fell backwards and put her pillow over her face.

"Hey, come on, Sophie, I'm your brother," Thad said.

"That's why she's embarrassed." Nora took Sophie by the arm and pulled her to a seated position. "Come on. Sit up."

"It's not a big deal," Thad said. "You'll be fine."

"Everyone treats it like a big deal," Sophie said glumly.

"A girl in her class named Destiny is giving her a hard time about it," Nora said.

"All I need is two key words," said Sophie.

"That's easy," Thad said. "*Hormones* and *glands*."

"*Hormones* and *glands*," Sophie repeated.

"Thad, are you sure . . . ?" Nora said doubtfully.

"Relax." Thad perched on the stool at Sophie's art table. "Sophie has the right to know. After all, she's . . . what are you now, Soph, eleven?"

"Ten."

"Ten, then."

"And you're going to be the one to tell her?" Nora slowly shook her head. "I'm not sure I can stick around for this."

"Nora, please," Sophie cried when Nora stood up. "Don't leave me."

"Let me give you a simple analogy," said Thad. He was preparing for the college PSATs and had been walking around the house spouting analogies for weeks. "Hormones are to a body as gas is to a car."

"A car?" Nora slowly sat back down. "This I have to hear."

"It's very simple, Soph." Thad leaned forward with his elbows on his knees. "When you're a baby, you're really happy, right? You don't have to worry about a thing. You crawl around all day, saying 'goo-goo' and 'ga-ga,' and when you're wet, some-one changes your diaper, and when you're hungry, someone feeds you. You with me so far?"

All Sophie could do was nod. Even Nora was silent.

"Little kids are happy too. They get to dig in the sandbox and make up weird superhero or prin-cess games, and someone cooks for them and tucks them into bed at night. The toughest job they have is learning how to tie their shoes." Thad was really getting into this. "So, you've got all these little kids running around, having a good time, waving sticks, pretending to be heroes and playing on the jungle gym and the swings, without a care in the world. But what's going to happen if they don't grow up?"

Thad paused, as if waiting for an answer. Sophie looked at him blankly.

"The world's going to be filled with five- and six-year olds, that's what," Thad said. "They can't hold jobs . . . they can't drive . . . they've never heard of algebra . . . Who's going to run for president?"

Nora's mouth fell open.

"Big problem, right?" Thad shook his head.

"So your brain says, 'I've got to do something to rev up these kids or they're never going to grow up! They're going to want to stay young forever!'"

Sophie was mesmerized.

"It's the same thing with a car," Thad said. "If it weren't for gas, a car would stand still. Sometimes, you've got to put your pedal to the metal and gun it or you're going to run into that ditch or hit the little old lady who's taking her sweet time in the crosswalk when you're late for school. That's what hormones are for."

"No wonder Mom didn't want you to drive," said Nora.

"So you're saying that hormones are gasoline?" Sophie said.

"Heck no! That would kill us. Hormones *act* like gasoline."

"Where do they come from?" said Sophie.

"That's where glands come in. They're like these—I don't know—little . . . little kind of marshmallow-shaped pillows, scattered around your body." Thad gestured vaguely in the area of his chest. "When a kid's ten, eleven, twelve . . . the brain goes, 'Let's gun it! This kid likes being a kid too much!' and the glands squirt out this hormone stuff, and weird things start growing in weird places, and one minute you're happy but the next minute you're crying if you're a girl, or if you're a boy, you want to buy a motorcycle or punch someone out."

Sophie and Nora were both staring at him, slack-jawed.

Thad looked pleased that he'd held their attention so well. "Everybody needs hormones so they can gun it through high school and college, until before they know it, they're boring, middle-aged people who have to work to feed their kids. It's as simple as that." Thad slapped his hands on his knees and pushed himself to a standing position. "Any questions?"

"That's it?" Sophie said. "*Hormones* and *glands*? That's all I have to say to make Alice happy and Destiny leave me alone?"

"You got it." His job finished, Thad headed for the door. "I'm telling you, Sophie, they'll think you're an expert. *Bye-bye, Destiny*." Thad wiggled the fingers of one hand. "You can take it from there, Nora," he said, and was gone.

"Well," Nora said. She didn't say anything else for a minute. "How did that sound?"

"Good," said Sophie. "I mean, I know that's not exactly how the whole thing works—your body and everything—but it was good."

"It's close enough for now." Nora got up. "You know, I have a book Mom gave me. If you want to look at it, I can give it to you."

"Thanks a lot, but no thanks," Sophie said quickly. The last thing she wanted was more information. What she didn't know, she wouldn't have to repeat. Out loud, in front of a crowd.

"I don't blame you. You've always been kind of clueless and happy in your own little world, Sophie. Now that I think about it," Nora said with a laugh, "so was I. I might still be there if it weren't for hormones." She stopped at Sophie's door. "Well, it's in my room when you want it. Maybe I should hide it so you can sneak around, looking through all my personal stuff, the way you used to."

"I don't do things like that anymore," said Sophie.

"Yeah, right." Nora stepped into the hallway but then quickly turned around. "Oh, and tell the girls at your meeting not to wish for big boobs. I've heard they're heavy." And then Nora was gone too.

Sophie got up in a daze and walked over to her art table and sat down.

Her brain was a confusion of marshmallows and gas pedals and five-year-olds sitting behind the desk in the Oval Office. But what Thad had said didn't feel at all embarrassing. That's what was so amazing. And the part about everything suddenly speeding up, and people being happy one minute and miserable the next, made sense.

How do you know when hormones start? Sophie wondered. Maybe they were flowing through her body right now. She never used to let girls like Destiny bother her. Maybe her hormones were allergic to Destiny's hormones.

Or wasn't that how it worked?

Maybe you could feel it when the glands squirted them out. Like a squirt gun.

Sophie sat very still to see if she could feel anything.

Nope. Nothing.

Phew.

Nora had offered to give her the book. Sophie

wouldn't have to steal it. When she was ready for it, she could walk right up to Nora's room and borrow it.

But not yet.

Mrs. Dubowski wasn't much taller than Sophie but she was twice as wide. She wore bright red lipstick and her gray hair piled into a bun on top of her head like a swirl of frosting on a cupcake.

In addition to the stuffed cabbage, she'd brought a delicious Polish dessert called something that sounded like "hroosh-cheeky." The pastries looked like bow ties covered with powdered sugar. Mrs. Dubowski said the name was spelled *chrusciki* and made them practice saying it correctly before she would let them eat one.

John couldn't get it right, but Mrs. Dubowski relented because he was little. John put the palms of his hands together, bowed, and said, "White Tiger thanks you very much," in such a dignified way that Mrs. Dubowski told him he could have as many as he wanted. "Even Thad's?" said John. Thad quickly licked his, which made them all laugh.

Both the chrusciki and the stuffed cabbage

were delicious. No one had to pretend when they said nice things.

When Mr. Hartley told her about the date with five chaperones, Mrs. Dubowski laughed and laughed.

"If I brought my grandson with me, that would make six," she said.

"It sounds like a movie," said Sophie.

"Or a sitcom," said Nora.

It was only when her dad and Mrs. Dubowski started talking about how to get stains out of laundry that Sophie excused herself and went upstairs. It had been a long week. She would be happy when her mother got home.

For tonight, she had her two words: *hormones* and *glands*. Nothing embarrassing about those. All she needed now was a sunny day tomorrow so that Nora's hair would behave on her date, and they would all be happy.

NINE

Sophie woke up the next morning to the sound of rain.

Oh, no.

She sat up.

Today was Friday. Tonight was Sammy's party.

Sophie leaped out of bed and hurried down the hall to the bathroom just as Nora yanked open the door. "Don't talk to me," she snarled. She brushed past Sophie with the hair dryer and brush in hand, stomped down the hall, and slammed the door to the attic behind her.

Sophie sighed.

This was crazy.

This was absolutely ridiculous.

Sophie *hated* hair. Hair was boring!

"Boring, boring, boring!" she shouted.

Great! And now she was getting upset about

hair after she'd made a list and memorized it and had gone around repeating it to herself again and again. She'd *promised* herself she would never get upset about the stupid subject, and here she was yelling about it.

And it wasn't even her hair!

"Dad?" Sophie called, stomping down the hall to her parents' bedroom.

"I'm in here."

The Hartleys' room was a mess. The bed was covered with heaps of clean, unfolded laundry. The dirty sheets Mr. Hartley had stripped off the bed were piled on the floor, along with the blankets and the quilt. All of the drawers in Mr. Hartley's dresser were gaping open, and several pairs of his sweatpants hung over the back of a chair.

Maura was sitting on the floor of the closet, putting on Mrs. Hartley's high heels.

"I don't know how your mother does it," Mr. Hartley said, running his hands through his hair. It looked as if he'd been caught in a windstorm. "I don't know how she takes care of all of you, and holds down a job, and cooks and cleans and does the laundry! All at the same time! Every time

I turned around all week, there were more dirty clothes!"

"I know. You told Mrs. Dubowski last night," Sophie said.

"And then the dust!" her dad went on. "Mom will be home tomorrow and I promised her the house would be clean, but every time I walk into the family room, there's dust and junk everywhere!"

"Dad," Sophie said.

"And shoes and socks! Hasn't anyone in this family heard of closets?"

"Dad!"

Mr. Hartley stopped ranting and looked at her. "What?"

"There's a problem."

"You're telling me."

"No, I mean about the weather. Tonight is Nora's date. She's going to be a wreck about her hair."

"That's another thing! Nora's hair!" Mr. Hartley sagged onto a pile of laundry on the bed like a balloon that was losing its air. "It's too much. It's all too much for one person to handle. What do I know about hair?"

It was a good thing their mom didn't get as emotional about the stuff she had to do. Her dad was clearly losing his grip. He needed calming down.

"It's okay," Sophie said. She patted his back as she sat down beside him. "The thing is, all Nora has wanted for the past few months is to get her hair straightened. She's asked Mom a million times, but Mom says it's too expensive and that curly hair is wonderful and Nora should be proud of hers."

"Well, she should be," said Mr. Hartley. "My mother had curly hair and she was beautiful. Look at her." He gestured to the photograph of Mr. and Mrs. Witherspoon on his dresser. "I never once heard my mom talk about straightening her hair," he said. "She was proud of it. I agree with Mom. Nora should be proud of hers, too."

"Dad!"

Sophie had to stop him now or he'd go on and on. She wasn't even dressed for school yet.

"It doesn't matter what you and Mom think," she said. "What matters is what Nora thinks. All the people in the world can think you're wonderful, but if you don't feel wonderful, it doesn't help."

Her dad looked at her for a minute. "I guess you're right," he said with a sigh.

"I *am* right," Sophie said. "If Nora's hair looks terrible tonight, it will ruin her memory of her first date for the rest of her life. And when Mom gets home, Nora will be an absolute wreck and she'll blame the whole thing on Mom and they'll get into a big fight about it and it will be like Mom never went away."

"Okay, okay, I get your point." Her dad smiled at her. "I guess you're a little tired of the subject too."

"I wish people were all bald. Then no one would have anything to complain about."

"Knowing people, they'd start complaining about sunburned scalps." The idea seemed to cheer up Mr. Hartley. "And about the glare of the sun reflecting off so many bald heads! They'd blame traffic accidents on it! What a picture, Sophie."

Sophie stood up.

"Can I tell Nora you'll take her to the hairdresser after school?"

"I guess so."

"Thanks."

"Where have you been?" Alice cried, rushing up to Sophie when she got to school. Jenna trailed behind her, spinning her yo-yo. "It's almost time for the bell to ring," Alice said.

"My dad's freaking out because Mom's coming home tomorrow and the house is a mess, and Nora was having a fit because it's raining and she has a . . . oh, forget it." Sophie opened the door and led Alice and Jenna through.

"I thought you said your dad was doing a great job," Jenna said.

"He was, at first. I think it wore him out. I'm not sure men are so good at the children-laundry-cooking thing if it goes on for too long."

"Did you find the book?" said Alice.

"Not exactly," said Sophie.

"What does that mean?" Alice said, her voice rising a little.

"Alice!" Jenna said. "Calm down."

"Trust me, Alice. It's going to be fine," Sophie said. "Have we ever let each other down?"

"No," Alice said.

"So, do you feel better?"

"No."

"Boy, will I be glad when this meeting is over," Jenna said to Sophie in a low voice.

"You and me both."

"Any questions?" Sophie asked.

The girls who were huddled around Sophie shook their heads. They had gathered after recess in an alcove off the hallway to the cafeteria and listened to Sophie with rapt attention.

"What you said was good," Caroline said.

"*Cars* and *gas*," said Gabriella. "Well, really *hormones* and *glands,* but I like *cars* and *gas* better."

The other girls nodded.

Jenna had been keeping an eye out for their class among the groups filing past them on their way to the cafeteria. She ducked back into the alcove and said, "I think I see them."

"We'd better go," Sophie said.

"I don't think being twelve will be too bad," Megan said as they moved into the hall. "My older sister wears really pretty bras. They have lace and everything."

"Oh. That reminds me." Sophie stopped and

turned to face them. "Don't wish for big boobs. They're heavy."

Whirling back around, Sophie nearly collided with Mrs. Stearns. Her teacher took a quick step back and raised her right eyebrow ever so slightly—so minutely that Sophie was never sure afterward that it had actually happened—before continuing down the hall.

"Omigod!" Caroline gasped. "She heard you!" The group dissolved into giggles, falling against one another and shrieking.

"I knew the immature girls would go to your meeting." It was Destiny. She and Hailey stopped as their class filed past. "You probably didn't even say anything important because everyone was too embarrassed to listen."

"If anyone's immature, it's you," said Sophie. "We're not the ones who're running around whispering about a movie about the human body."

Destiny blinked. Hailey looked at her for direction, but there wasn't any.

"In my family, the body's no more embarrassing or complicated than a car," Sophie said.

"A car?" said Destiny.

"I have a book, in case you two need to read it," Alice said.

"And I have three older brothers, which is even better." Jenna spun out her yo-yo and yanked it back up again. "You wouldn't *believe* what I've learned being around them."

"Really?" said Hailey.

"Hailey!" said Destiny.

"We can find out everything we want to know on our own, okay?" Sophie said. "So just *back off*." John would have been proud of her.

For a moment, Destiny was speechless. She looked around distractedly, as if searching for a different target. "Don't you think you're a little old to be playing with a yo-yo?" she said to Jenna.

"What does age have to do with anything?" Jenna said.

"Fine." Destiny flicked her ponytail with enough energy that it would have wiped the entire group off the face of the earth if it had connected. "Be that way. Come on, Hailey."

"I don't think Destiny's going to bug us anymore," Jenna said. "At least, not about that."

Her yo-yo was spinning inches above the floor. When Jenna lowered it enough so that it touched the ground, it rolled away from her as if it were running down the hall, until she jerked her hand and made it run back up the string.

"That's called 'walk the dog,'" she said proudly.

"And what we just did is called 'getting rid of Destiny,'" said Sophie.

"Relax your feet . . . relax your legs . . ." Ms. Bell's quiet voice slowly floated through the gym. "Relax your stomach . . . relax your hands . . . let your whole body relax . . ."

Sophie lay with her eyes closed and her hands at her sides. Her body felt limp, like a strand of spaghetti. Or maybe more like a car when you turn off the ignition and it stops moving and goes still.

My body, my body, my body, Sophie thought. She didn't feel the least bit embarrassed.

TEN

"Bye! Have a great time! Have her home by ten, Ian." Mr. Hartley shut the door behind Nora and Ian and leaned heavily against it. "Thank heavens that's over."

"He kind of mumbled," Sophie said, sitting on the couch. "I mean, he was nice and everything, but I couldn't understand what he was saying."

"That's because his hair covered up his face," said John.

"Not his whole face, John," said Mr. Hartley. "Only his eyes."

"And half his nose," said Sophie.

Mr. Hartley pushed himself away from the door. "Well! I don't know about you two, but I feel much better now that Nora has been launched."

"Good thing she's not here to hear you. You make her sound like a ship," Sophie said. "That was a good call, not making her eat dinner. I think she really would have thrown up."

"Come on, Dad, you promised." John held out his hand, palm up. "I didn't try to kick him or ambush him."

"A deal's a deal," Mr. Hartley agreed. He pulled some bills out of his pocket, peeled off a single for John, and gave it to him. John promptly ran upstairs to hide it.

"You bribed him?" Sophie said indignantly. "How come you didn't bribe me?"

"I knew you had too much integrity to accept a bribe," her dad said. "You can choose tonight's movie—how's that?"

"Tonight's movie and *you* have to make the popcorn," Sophie said.

"Deal. But I'm telling you one thing right now, Sophie," said Mr. Hartley. "There's a new rule in this family, starting with you: no dating until you're thirty."

"Deal," said Sophie.

Sophie was packing for a sleepover at Alice's house the next day when John called up the stairs.

"Mom's home!"

Sophie finished stuffing the last of her things into her suitcase and zipped it closed. After giving Patsy a quick kiss on the head, she headed for the stairs as Nora came down the hall behind her.

"Hurry up, slowpoke. I'm dying to see what Mom says about my hair." Nora gave Sophie a playful prod in the back.

"She probably won't even notice," said Sophie.

At the bottom of the stairs, Maura was toddling down the hall to the kitchen. Sophie swooped her up and carried her into the kitchen as the mudroom door opened and Mr. Hartley came in carrying Mrs. Hartley's suitcase.

"Mommy home?" said Maura. Then Mrs. Hartley appeared in the doorway behind her husband, and Maura's eyes opened wide. Her thumb fell out of her mouth as she wailed, "Mommy home!" and burst into tears.

"Maura, sweetie," said Mrs. Hartley. She took Maura from Sophie and hugged her tight, patting her back and kissing her. "Don't cry, Maura. Mommy's home."

"She was fine the whole time, Mom, really," Nora said.

"She didn't cry once," said Sophie.

"Dad almost cried last night when he burned the hamburgers and the buns caught fire in the toaster oven," reported John.

"Now, John, no tattling." Mr. Hartley put his arm around his wife's shoulders. "But I have to confess: I did almost cry when I saw the airport van pull into the driveway just now."

They all laughed.

"We missed you, honey," Mr. Hartley said. "I don't know how you do it. It's much easier to carry thousands of pounds of other people's junk in and out of houses."

"I don't know how you travel as much as you do," said Mrs. Hartley. "I can hardly wait to sleep in my own bed again."

"I think we did pretty well, though. Didn't we, kids?" said Mr. Hartley.

"I have to admit, Dad was great," Nora said. "We were a little worried we were going to see chicken chow mein every night, but we didn't. Not even once."

Mrs. Hartley looked closely at Nora. "What did you do to your hair?"

"I had it professionally blow-dried yesterday," Nora said. She shook her head back and forth to make her straight hair fly out around her. "I wanted to get it straightened, but Dad said I had to wait until you were home. Besides, I checked, and hair straightening is so expensive! Dad treated me to the blow dry, and I bought a round brush the stylist recommended. She showed me how to do this myself. I love it."

"It looks very nice," Mrs. Hartley said, "and if it makes you happy, that's wonderful. How was your date?"

"Great! But I'll have to tell you tomorrow." Nora looked at the clock and started moving toward the door. "Kate's mom is picking me up in about ten minutes. We're going to play practice and then I'm spending the night at her house."

"Have fun," Mrs. Hartley called to Nora's disappearing back.

She sat at the table with Maura in her lap and sighed. "It's so nice to be home. Tom, would you get me a glass of water, please? Where's Thad?"

"Playing soccer. After that, he's going bowling with friends. And after *that*," Mr. Hartley said, handing the water to his wife, "he's going over to his new girlfriend's house."

"What happened to Emily?" said Mrs. Hartley.

"Long story. I'll tell you later."

"How are you, Sophie?" Mrs. Hartley said. "I see you're headed out too."

"Jenna and I are spending the night at Alice's. First I have to change Patsy's litter box, and then I have to eat lunch. Want me to make you a sandwich?" Sophie put her suitcase next to the back door and went to open the cabinets.

"Thanks, but I bought a sandwich in the airport and ate it on the plane. Well," Mrs. Hartley said, as Maura held tight to her mother's necklace and contentedly sucked her thumb, "it certainly seems that everyone's in good shape and spirits around here. It's lovely to be home."

"It's lovely to have you," said Mr. Hartley.

When they kissed, John clutched his neck and made gagging noises. "Dad wasn't all lovey-dovey when you weren't here," he said disgustedly.

"I'm glad to hear that, John," said Mrs. Hartley.

She sniffed the air. "Don't tell me you've even been baking, Tom."

"John and I made brownies," Mr. Hartley said. "Come on, let's go sit in the family room so you can be comfortable. I want to hear about the conference."

"And I want to hear about what went on here."

"The brownies are for tonight!" John announced, leaping around in front of his parents like an excited puppy as he led the way down the hall. "We're going to eat brownies and play Candy Land. The whole family."

"It looks to me as if the older children are busy, John," Mrs. Hartley said. "But you and Maura and Dad and I will have a good time."

"Yes, John, the *older* children are busy," Sophie said. She tried to toss her hair the way Nora had done, but it was too curly to move as easily. "Darn you, Mrs. Witherspoon," she said haughtily as she opened a can of tuna fish. "It's all your fault."

"I have to ask one more thing," Alice said.

"*Al*-ice," Jenna said impatiently. "Your five minutes are up."

They were in Alice's bedroom, plotting what to do for the night. Sophie was sprawled on one of the twin beds. Jenna was rewinding her yo-yo for the millionth time.

"But—" Alice protested.

"We're done talking about it!" Jenna shouted.

"Please . . . ?"

"Go on, Alice. What?" Sophie said.

"Okay, if our bodies are like a car, then what's our brain?" said Alice.

Jenna sighed loudly.

Sophie thought for a second. "The steering wheel," she said.

"Oh. That makes sense. What about our heart?"

"That's two things," Jenna said.

"Your heart's like the engine," Sophie said.

"So that means our feet are like the tires?" Alice said dubiously.

"Be quiet! Be quiet! Be quiet!" Jenna yelled, jumping up and down and waving her hands in the air. "We said no more questions! "You're an idiot!" she shouted. Jenna grabbed a pillow and hurled it at Alice, who hurled one back. All three of them started throwing pillows, laughing and shouting like crazy people.

When they were exhausted, they lay on the beds.

"Let's make a pact," Sophie said. "No more talking about P-U until next year."

"I second it," said Jenna.

"Okay. But I feel better about it, don't you?" Alice said happily.

"I feel like cheese," Jenna said.

"Eating cheese," Sophie agreed, "and then putting on music and dancing."

"Okay. And then maybe we can take pictures of ourselves with the new camera my dad gave me," Alice said.

"I need one of the three of us," said Sophie. "And I want each of us to be wearing one of the tie-dyed things you made."

"Those nerdy things?" said Jenna.

"Okay, but first, let's go get the cheese." Alice stopped with her hand on the doorknob. "Just one last thing," she said quickly. "We won't talk about it again unless two of us feel like talking about it, and then we can as long as we don't include the other person."

Another barrage of pillows put an end to the conversation.

"What's this?" said Mrs. Hartley the following evening.

"This way, my-dam," John said formally. He stuck out his elbow for his mother to hold and led her into the dining room. With his other hand, he held up the bottom of the suit jacket he'd taken from Mr. Hartley's closet to wear over his underwear, so he wouldn't trip.

Thad, Sophie, and Nora had Googled "basic table manners." The men were supposed to stay standing until the women sat down. Now Thad was standing behind his chair in a jacket and tie, waiting for his mother to sit down before he did.

"Fat chance around here," Nora had said when they'd read it. She was wearing the sequined jacket and the new skirt she'd worn on her date, her new platform shoes, and her new straight hair.

Sophie had on her tiara, the one Nora had

given her when she was nine. Sophie hadn't worn it in a while, and she had forgotten how it brought out her regal, queenly side. She planned on sitting up straight and talking with an English accent all through dinner.

She and Nora had set the dining-room table using the best china and silverware, a tablecloth, and candles. They put out wineglasses and a bottle of wine for Mr. and Mrs. Hartley, too. Mr. Hartley had even bought a cake. It had "Welcome Home" written on the top, surrounded by balloons. It sat on the sideboard, ready for dessert.

"We planned a special welcome-home dinner for you," said Mr. Hartley. He pulled out the chair at one end of the table. "Please, sit down. I'll be right out with the dinner."

Mr. Hartley came back carrying a meat loaf on Mrs. Hartley's best platter. It was surrounded by a sea of mashed potatoes studded with peas.

"John insisted," said Mr. Hartley.

"I decorated it," said John. "The peas are people drowning after a shipwreck."

"Meat loaf again?" Sophie said. Then she caught

herself and gave a polite cough. "I mean, I say! Meat loaf again! Jolly good!"

Nora rolled her eyes but all she said was, "So, Mother. How was your conference? Did you find it productive?"

"Yes, Nora," Mrs. Hartley said. "Very productive. Thank you."

There was a lull in the conversation.

"We had a very productive week at home, too, didn't we, Thad darling?" Nora said encouragingly.

"Thad darling?" Mrs. Hartley mouthed to Mr. Hartley.

Thad frowned to have the ball suddenly lobbed into his court, but then he gamely smiled and said, "Very productive."

"Mine was very, very, very productive," said John.

"I think we've had enough productivity for the week," said Mr. Hartley.

Thad sat up quickly, as if struck with a sudden inspiration. "I think we should let Mother talk about her conference," he said gallantly.

"What did you *do* to them?" Mrs. Hartley asked Mr. Hartley in a low voice.

"I'm tired of the conference," John said. "Dad let me brush my teeth in the bathtub every night. The water had the dirt from my feet and everything."

"John!" said Nora. "Your manners!"

"How wonderfully hygienic, Tom," Mrs. Hartley said.

"Yes," said Sophie, "and Thad, I have to thank you for doing such a good job of explaining the facts of life to me."

"Thad told you *the facts of life?*" Mrs. Hartley said in a faint voice.

"And you, Nora, for warning me about big bosoms."

Thad choked and spewed out his milk. It sprayed all over Nora. "Thad! You slob!" Nora shouted as Thad bolted for the bathroom with the tail of his tie held over his mouth. She jumped to her feet, knocking over her chair, and dabbed furiously at her clothes with her napkin. "This is my new skirt, you idiot! You ruined it! Oh, and my jacket, too!" she cried, hurling her napkin onto the table. "I hate you, I hate you, I hate you!"

She ran out of the room.

"Bosoms!" John shouted. He fell off his chair and onto the floor, where he rolled around, pounding the rug with his fists and shouting, "Sophie said *bosoms!*"

"Back off!" Maura cried, peering with interest at John over the tray of her highchair. She picked up a pea from her dish and put it into her mouth. Then she picked up another pea and dropped it over the edge. "You big bully," she said.

Mrs. Hartley and Mr. Hartley stared at each other in amazement.

"What went on while I was gone?" said Mrs. Hartley.

"Apparently, more than I realized," said Mr. Hartley.

Her mom didn't sound mad, but Sophie wasn't taking any chances. "You should do what I do, Mom, and become a tree. It makes it much easier." Sophie got up and stood near the sideboard. Steadying her tiara with one hand, she rested her left foot against her right leg and hummed, "Ommm . . ."

"Bosoms!" said John. Maura dropped another pea.

Mr. Hartley gave his wife a weak smile.

"Sorry," he said. "It fell apart a little sooner than I had hoped."

"I'm kind of relieved," Mrs. Hartley said. "I was beginning to think the children had been abducted by aliens and replaced with robots."

"And we wouldn't want that?" Mr. Hartley said hopefully.

"Bosoms," John croaked. He was running out of steam.

When Maura dropped another pea, it pushed the Hartley parents over the edge. They burst out laughing. Sophie couldn't remember ever seeing them laugh as hard. Mrs. Hartley had to use her napkin to wipe the tears from her eyes, and Mr. Hartley took off his glasses and used the back of his hand. Every time it seemed they might stop, John gasped, "Bosoms," and Maura dropped another pea.

It was impossible to become a tree under these conditions.

"Honestly," Sophie said, putting her foot on the floor. "If you two act so immature about the word *bosoms*, I don't know how you ever managed to have children."

This sent her parents off on another gale of laughter.

Let them laugh, Sophie thought, straightening her tiara. Obviously she was the only mature person in the entire family. Even if no one else had any self-control, *she* was going to carry on with the meal.

Sophie picked up the cake and put it on the table in front of her chair. She sat down, took her knife, cut herself a slice that went from the *W* to the *o* and encompassed three balloons, and put it onto her plate.

"Jolly good," Sophie said, and dug in.